SATURNALIA

A TALE OF WICKEDNESS AND
REDEMPTION IN ANCIENT ROME

Adam Alexander Haviaras

Cover designed by LLPix Designs

*Please note: To enhance the reader's experience, there is a glossary of Latin words at the back of this book.

JOIN THE LEGIONS!

Sign-up for the Eagles and Dragons Publishing
Newsletter and get a FREE BOOK today.

Subscribers get first access to new releases,
special offers, and much more.

Go to:
www.eaglesanddragonspublishing.com

and this story is, perhaps, one of the best I've ever read."

"An outstanding and compelling novel!"

"I would add this author to some of the great historical writers such as Conn Iggulden, Simon Scarrow and David Gemmell. The characters were described in such a way that it was easy to picture them as if they were real and have lived in the past, the book flowed with an ease that any reader, novice to advanced can enjoy and become fully immersed..."

"One in a series of tales which would rank them alongside Bernard Cornwell, Simon Scarrow, Robert Ludlum, James Boschert and others of their ilk. The story and character development and the pacing of the exciting military actions frankly are superb and edge of your seat! The historical environment and settings have been well researched to make the story lines so very believable!! I can hardly wait for what I hope will be many sequels! If you enjoy Roman historical fiction, you do not want to miss this series!"

Goodreads:

"... a very entertaining read; Haviaras has both a fluid writing style, and a good eye for historical detail, and explores in far more detail the faith of the average Roman than do most authors."

For my family...

SATURNALIA

A TALE OF WICKEDNESS AND
REDEMPTION IN ANCIENT ROME

PREFACE

An ancient papyrus has come to me by means I cannot disclose. Suffice it to say that, upon my translation of this ancient tale, sleep has eluded me, and every movement in the shadows reminds me of the horrors set down upon that brittle reed paper.

The man you shall read about in these pages could be any person known to you or me, so long as he had a heart of stone and merited the wrath of Heaven and Hell.

It is undoubtedly safe to assume that most of you who come across this book are familiar with that long-standing classic, *A Christmas Carol*, by Mr. Charles Dickens.

Indeed, his tale has not only entertained many who make merry at Christmastime, but also shaped the ways in which people celebrate it. Upon hearing the title of that story, one immediately scents roast meats and fresh, steaming breads, or tastes the sweetest of nectars in one's throat, or smacks one's lips at the sight of delicacies piled high upon candlelit tables.

Or perhaps you instead have an inkling of dread at the memory of three spirits, those sent to haunt the wicked Ebenezer Scrooge? And too right! It is a tale of terror and redemption that brings about the true, forgive me…spirit…of Christmas.

Now, hold fast, dear reader, while I tell you something you likely do not know.

There is another tale, a much more ancient tale of wickedness and horror that would chill the very marrow of your bones were you brave enough to read it.

It is a tale of ancient Rome and of a man who lived there centuries ago, if 'living' you could call it.

This man's name was Catus Pompilius, and never a more unfeeling, unfaithful man has walked the earth before or since the time in which this tale unfolds.

If you are resolved to hear this tale of dread, of shades and furies, and of gods, then do read on by the glow of a bright light, for it will guide you in the darkness into which you are about to throw yourself.

We go back now to the year A.D. 203 in the city of imperial Rome, and the festival of Saturnalia, when most citizens' spirits were high and their cups were overflowing with kindness…

I

A DOMUS OF DEATH

The Gods do not demand much of Man. The occasional offering or prayer, a bit of a nod on the appropriate festival day, respect toward their representatives at temples and altars where their own particular rites are performed.

In the broad scheme of this life, the truth is that Man can get away with doing very little. In fact, it is common knowledge that those who do not do honour to the life they have been given, who reign cruelly over others, often get away with it. It is those honest citizens who seem to bear the brunt of others' actions.

Some might think that the Gods did not exist for all that the wicked run away with...but they would be wrong.

The Gods do indeed take notice. They walk among

us…judge us. It might take a lifetime for them to take action, but when they do… Well, it casts a long dark shadow to think on it.

One thing you can be sure of is that when the Gods do take action, they do so with greater cruelty than any mortal is capable of, and it is more often than not the worst of our species upon whom they visit their savage lessons.

I tell you now a tale of a man, the cruelest wretch in all of Rome, and the time, one winter, that he underwent such an ordeal as to slash the skin from your bones and freeze your marrow.

This man's name was Catus Pompilius.

It began the year that Emperor Severus was away from Rome, luxuriating in the glow of his home province of Africa Proconsularis and that gem of the South, Leptis Magna.

On the eve of the great festival of Saturnalia, this Catus Pompilius left the east wing of his villa on the Esquiline Hill to begin his daily work of collecting rents, evicting hard-working Romans, and insulting every client who came to his door, a door he shared with his partner in cruelty, Krelis Manvilio. Both men rejected family or anything having to do with warmth and kindness.

They were landlords, Catus and Krelis, and it was their business to lord it over rich and poor alike across all of Rome. There was no building they did not have a stake in, no matter how ornate or humble.

Together, Catus and Krelis had taken this rather large villa on the edges of the gardens of Maecenas from one of their debtors, a merchant who had had some success and soon thereafter decided to build a great villa on that fashionable hill of Rome. Well, Fortuna was not to linger with this merchant, and so his sprawling villa went to the two business partners. It became their domus and place of business all in one.

On the morning of that one eve of Saturnalia, Catus came downstairs to find Krelis lying at the bottom of the stairs in the west wing of the villa which belonged to Krelis.

Catus stood there, his mind calm, calculating the way in which such a thing could have happened.

"Drunk, one last time," he said to the sprawled body, the corner of one side of his wrinkled and ridged face curling up as if reaching for a smile. "Serves you right. And it serves me just fine."

Catus stepped over the body, avoiding the pool of blood that had formed around Krelis' cracked skull, crossed the dark atrium to the latter's own tablinum, and returned with a heavy wooden chest of denarii which he transferred to his own rooms. After three more such trips, he turned back to the body of his business partner and shook his head.

"You've certainly made some work for me now, haven't you? Now I shall not get as much done today as I had planned." He looked around the atrium, then to the front door where a stool sat nearby, empty. "Giles!" he yelled for the man who worked for him as a rent collector.

He went angrily to the door and threw it open to look up and down the tree clad street.

In the distance, Catus spotted the brawny figure of the ex-gladiator striding quickly toward the villa. "You're late!" he hissed at the man.

"Sorry, sir. My little Diana took sick this morning and I had to run for a medicus."

Catus grabbed hold of the bigger man and jabbed a bony fist into his chest. "Your little family problems are none of my concern! You hear me? You owe me a debt, Giles, and if you're not careful and attentive to your duty to me, I can have you pay off that debt in the amphitheatre again. It's only been one year since you left the sands."

"There'll be no need for that," the big man said calmly, his chest rising and falling as he looked down at Catus.

"Good. Now get inside. There's something you have to take care of."

Giles walked through the front door into the atrium where the grey morning light lit upon the twisted body and bleeding head of Krelis. He turned round on Catus, shock in his eyes.

"It wasn't me who did it, you imbecile!"

"I didn't say it was, sir. But…"

"But what?"

"He was your friend and partner of many years. What a tragedy!" Giles turned back to kneel beside the body, the blank, once-mean eyes now vacant and lonely.

"The only tragedy," Catus said, "is that I shall have to do double the work and pick up the slack." His scornful eyes lingered on the body for a moment before he began to walk back to his own tablinum. "Get it out of here, Giles, before the clients begin to arrive."

"But, sir, shouldn't we close for the day out of respect for the dead?"

Catus' form stopped at the threshold to his office on the other side of the atrium. He turned slowly, his eyes black in the shadows.

"Business will continue as usual, Giles."

"I'll need money for the undertaker, mourners, and the mason to carve a stele for the necropolis."

At the mention of the expenditures, Catus' face contorted in anger, more so than at the death of his business partner, for he valued money above all things, above reason, above comfort, above goodness, and even above life itself. He went into his tablinum and came back with a small leather pouch, the contents of which he poured out into the palm of his hand.

Giles watched as Catus counted out several bronze ases and a few sestercii.

Catus put them back in the pouch, clutching the others tightly in his hand, and then tossed the pouch to Giles.

"Have him burned and the ashes scattered beyond the city walls in the necropolis. I'm not paying for mourners or a monument. His funds shall remain with the business since he had no heirs."

"And the rites, sir? Surely his shade will rest better if some offerings are made at the temple for him?"

"What need has he for rites in Hades? Were it not illegal, I would simply have you dump his carcass outside the city walls for the dogs and carrion crows." He pointed at the pouch. "Do not spend all of that!"

"Yes, sir," Giles looked upon the man with fear then, not of physical retaliation, but for fear of what the Gods might do with one such as Catus, and what being in such close proximity to his employer might do to him.

"And you... After you finish getting rid of Krelis, you will go about your collections this evening as usual. There are many rents to collect."

"But it's the eve before Saturnalia, sir."

Catus stepped forward, his not inconsiderable patience, as he saw it, close to breaking point.

"Do I look like I give a fig leaf for Saturnalia, Giles? Do I?" His hard voice crashed upon the faded walls of the atrium, their once vibrant colour growing even sadder, the painted forest seeming to wilt and brown.

"The Dead to dine on Saturnalia!" he yelled.

Giles nodded, turned back to the body, and went to find an undertaker beneath the low-hanging sky of iron grey.

II

SHADES OF THE PAST

Every year with the arrival of the month of December there was an air of change, of hope in ancient Rome. No matter how desolate one's situation, or empty one's purse, the Gods seemed to infuse both citizen and slave with anticipation and joy.

This suffusion of jollity was no doubt closely tied to the great festival of Saturnalia when, even for a short time, life was better. As the poet once said, 'Saturnalia is the very best of days!'

In the days leading up to the seventeenth of December, everywhere you went among the seven hills, doorways were decorated with garlands. The homes of both rich and poor were brightly lit with myriad candles and lamps in those last, darkest days of the year.

The city and imperial fora were cleaned and

scrubbed in preparation for the array of games to be put on by the Senate, and the convivium publicum, the public feast that would follow the sacrifices to Saturn. The markets were all a chorus of buying and selling, the stalls brimming with freshly butchered meats, mountains of fruit and grain from the countryside, fish from the sea, and wines from Italia, Graecia and Gaul. The shipments of garum from Africa and Iberia tripled in order to meet the demand.

The entire city was a circus at which every person hoped for a share of joy, of food, and of the Gods' favour.

Token gifts, the sigillaria, were purchased in advance of the festival too, from the wax and tallow candles and figurines of the poor, to toys for children, clothing, lamps and writing tablets for those with a few extra denarii, all the way to exotic animals and pleasure slaves for the rich.

People prepared to set aside their togas in favour of the colourful, festive synthesis of Saturnalia, and the felt or leather pileus which men would wear atop their heads.

Oh, how the world was bright and lively at that time of year!

How all looked forward to these seven days from

the seventeenth of December to the twenty-third, the Dies Natalis Solis Invicti, the birthday of the unconquerable Sun, when the dark days of Winter would begin to burn away once more.

In addition to the permitted public gambling, the propensity for guising, overeating, and joyful drunkenness, the most exciting part of Saturnalia was the three days at the beginning of the festival when there was no work forced upon any person, when businesses and courts were shut, and schools and gymnasia closed.

The warlike people of Mars even refused to fight at this time of year, with no pilum or gladius raised against any enemy across the Empire.

This was a time to savour life, a time when master and slave exchanged places for even a day, the one served by the other, when kind words might be exchanged, and past wrongs perhaps forgiven, things made right.

From the emperor and empress who were far away, to the poorest family in the Suburra of Rome, there was a share of lightheartedness for each when the spirits would lift to the heights of Olympus at the hearing of that most wonderful of wishes, 'Io Saturnalia!'.

The Gods know the world is an imperfect place, but it must be admitted that it would indeed be better without certain people in it.

In Rome at the time, if you were to ask normal folk for the name of the most hated person, the name most likely to burst from their lips would not be that of the most brutal Aventine thug, or even the vilest and abusive wretch in the urban guard. No. The name of the person you would hear shouted with passionate hate would be that of Catus Pompilius.

Catus Pompilius was, one could say, the richest man in Rome. Some said that he was even wealthier than Marcus Licinius Crassus had been in his day. Everyone borrowed money from Catus Pompilius, not because it was preferred, but because he had much of it, and was not so choosy about whom he leant it to, whereas other lenders were. Everyone owed Pompilius: from the smallest butcher to the Praetorian Prefect, Papinianus, whom it was said needed extra funds to aid Emperor Severus in his imminent conquest of Caledonia.

He was also one of the wealthiest landlords in all of Rome, having used the funds he earned from interest, and the money he absconded from his dead partner, Krelis Manvilio, to buy up almost half of the city.

Most of his holdings consisted of the usual three

and five story tenements nestled in the Suburra of Rome, that poor and rough area tucked between the Viminal Hill, and the Esquiline Hill on which Pompilius lived, of course in a vast domus he had repossessed from a failed merchant's family.

Not even the Gods could save a debtor from Pompilius' bony clutches!

However, on that day, the Gods sitting in their Olympic eyrie took notice of the fiend as he stormed out of the Basilica Julia into the Forum Romanum.

Pompilius had just been to court on the eve of Saturnalia, only prior to its closing for the festival, to complete a suit against an olive oil importer from Hispania who had defaulted on a loan.

The man, now standing beneath the arcade of the basilica, shouting at Pompilius' back as he left, had told the magistrate that he would have the funds to fully repay the loan after Saturnalia, but Pompilius had refused and demanded that instead, all of the merchant's ships, stock, and real estate be transferred to him immediately.

This signed order he now rolled, as he strode through the Forum, and tucked it into the fold of his plain, grey toga.

Despite the crowds gathering to watch the preparations for the celebrations before the temple of Saturn and the convivium publicum where the people would dine at the expense of the Senate, a pathway cleared before Catus Pompilius' form as he pressed on. People avoided eye contact with the man at all cost, some even jostling to get far away from him, and not be called out.

Like a jungle predator, Catus Pompilius scanned the faces for people who owed him rents or other debts and, poor fellows, those whose arms he clamped onto were shivering with fright as the old man piled vitriol and shame upon them before their fellow citizens.

It was well-known how many men Catus had sent to the mines, or onto the merchant ships, to repay debts, how many families he had torn asunder for the price of a few denarii.

Some men of the patrician class stood their ground before the landlord and money-lender, staring down their long noses at him as though the Cloaca Maxima were in flow right beneath their snouts.

Yet he stared back, unperturbed, unafraid, and uncaring of any of them.

At a distance, if you did not know him, you would think Catus Pompilius simply a man of very advanced years, ignorant of his unclean appearance, and rude in his manner. He walked hunched over, as if constantly poring over his papyrus ledgers, so that the first thing one noticed was the top of his balding, spotted head flanked by the wings of his ears.

Harmless enough, until he raised his head like a vulture from a carcass to lay his eyes upon you, to assess you, to determine if you owed him something.

Until he took notice, all one saw was a face verily creased with bitterness and anger - the Gods alone knew at what! - the skin gathering in a great furrow above his brows as if his constant frown pulled the skin forward and down upon his face. Loose skin had also gathered about his large nose, which many said could scent coin the way a hound smells a bitch in heat. His mouth was turned down permanently, even when he spoke, so that the only sound he made was a low growl, his chin moving but a little.

This was Catus Pompilius, and on the eve of Saturnalia he was often at his worst, determined to ruin the circus atmosphere of the season and slap the smile from a thousand faces if he could.

They all owe me money, and yet they spend and spend and spend! he raged to himself as he strode along the tables being set out for the morrow's public banquet which would follow the ritus Graecus, the rituals in the Greek fashion that were performed at the temple of Saturn.

He hated everything about the festival - the waste of state funds on the profane citizenry, the giving of sigillaria, the guising, the public gambling, all of it! But most of all, he hated that hc was forced to give Giles Amadea, his collector, the first three days of the festival off, just like the rest of Rome, due to the ancient decree of dies festus.

That is why he needed an early start on the eve of Saturnalia every year, so that he could send Giles out to collect as many rents as he could before the coming of December seventeenth.

The sun was shining in the sky above as Pompilius made his way toward the slope of the Esquiline Hill, having already stopped at the markets of Trajan to gather rents from those who rented the blocks of stalls he had bought up, their rents having been due at the beginning of the month.

The gnarled branches of oak trees dotting the Esquiline Hill came into view, like claws rapping at the doors of the rich villas dotted around the plateau.

Catus turned onto his street and noted the garlands and flowers being hung at the doors of all of his neighbours, the polished herms, and well-dressed, happy slaves.

Of course they're happy! he snorted, *their fool masters will spend money on them and serve them a banquet like the idiots they are.*

One thing he could never understand was the kindness and generosity shown toward slaves at that time of year, for he strongly suspected that once the mongrels were given a little freedom to speak and do as they pleased, they would never again respect or fear their proper dominus.

"The Dead to dine on Saturnalia!" he cursed at the jolly slaves of his neighbour as he turned and put the key into the lock of his domus, opened the thick door, and slammed it shut so that the bronze gorgon-headed knocker echoed loudly on the quiet street.

"Ida!" he shouted in the dark, damp atrium. "Slave!"

From the back of the garden the sound of sweeping stopped suddenly and the shuffling footsteps moved in his direction.

"Yes, Dominus?" the answer came.

Ida was a middle-aged Ephesian woman whose family had sold her long ago to Catus, and for many years she had served him and Krelis Manvilio. She looked much older than her years upon the earth. She was thin, tired, and prematurely grey. Kindness was utterly foreign to her, having gone from one cruel house to another, though she forced herself to admit that her current situation could be much worse. At least Catus did not demand the certain other duties so many masters demanded of their female slaves.

He simply did not care.

"Make some broth for tonight," he growled, not looking at her.

"Yes, Dominus," she answered, hunched before him. "Would you care for meat in it? I could make you some fresh bread."

"Meat?" he snapped. "Costly it is! The inflated prices at this cursed time of year burden me! Absolutely not! And no bread either. I see your game," he poked her bony shoulder. "You would make some extra to keep for yourself. Always a glutton you are!"

"No bread. Yes, Dominus," Ida said, watching him march away to the tablinum on the other side of the atrium, the one formerly occupied by Krelis.

When Catus entered the tablinum, he turned abruptly, covering his eyes for all the brightness of the lamps lit by his employee, Giles Amadea.

"You do not need so much light!" Catus barked, going and blowing out three of the lamps, leaving only the one on the table that Giles used to read the lists he had found that morning on his table. "Oil is expensive!"

The room immediately faded to darkness with the extinguishing of the lights, the three gladii and two cudgels on the wall behind Giles going to shadow, and peeling, water-damaged plaster going black.

"So?" Catus snapped.

Giles Amadea was a large man who tolerated his employer's unforgivable manner for the meagre salary it afforded him and his family. Whenever Catus' voice would burst in upon his thoughts, the mantra *Anything is better than the bloody arena...* would repeat itself in his mind.

That thought normally brought him back to sense, cooling his frustration with Catus, but the last few years had been unbearable at best, and his daily trial of going to work had become a true hardship. Only thoughts of his family kept him from reaching for the gladius behind him and ending the old man. Rome would certainly have thanked him for it!

But Giles was a good man, his freedom in the arena

hard-won nine years before at the games in honour of Saturn, when bouts were to the death, an offering of blood to the chthonic god of seed-sowing.

He had tried making his living to support himself, his wife, Marcia, and their newborn daughter, Diana, but none would hire him, fearing to support a gladiator who had been meant as an offering to Saturn. The odds, had been highly stacked against him that day, long ago, when he had won his freedom.

A year after he had won his freedom, Catus and Krelis had hired him as a collector, during the hard times when war raged in the East, and people had become lax in paying their rents and debts.

Catus towered over the table, his shadowy eyes bearing down on Giles who looked up. "I asked you a question."

"Do we need to do this again?" Giles said.

Catus recoiled in disgust then slammed his bony hand on the table "YES!"

Giles stood behind the table, but Catus came around, his face up into his. "The problem with you, Giles, is you're too feeling...too sentimental. This is business! These are lists of people who have owed me money since the beginning of December and longer.

And yet, this very eve, they are out in the markets squandering my money...my money!... on sigillaria and food for a feast!"

"But, sir. It is Saturnalia. Wouldn't the Gods look kindly on your business if you were to give them some grace?"

Catus' face turned crimson, and the veins beneath his eyes bulged as he stared at the ex-gladiator.

"Do not speak to me of grace and the Gods...you idiot." His voice was low, menacing, like the tremors in the earth to the south of Rome. "And do not, I say, do not use Saturnalia as an excuse to shirk your work. I hired you for one thing, and one thing alone: to collect money and break bones. That is all. If you do not like your position, or the way I run my business, then you may leave my employ and crawl back to your Suburan hovel to try and scrape a living for your wife and five children. Do you hear me?"

Giles looked at the hateful man before him. *Anything is better than the bloody arena...* He nodded. "Yes, sir."

"That is your duty today...to collect rents from those on the lists, and if they do not pay, to forcibly evict them."

Catus turned and stormed back across the atrium to his own tablinum to go over his accounts profits and, how he hated them, losses.

Meanwhile, Giles went over the lists and felt his heart tighten at the day's prospects. Most of the people on those lists were his neighbours in the Suburra, some his friends. How could he possibly do this? He knew for a fact that they were not in the markets, spending away their rents on frivolities, but rather bartering services and skills, for meagre scraps to feed their families a little meat or cheese at Saturnalia. They carved toys for the day of the Sigillaria for their children out of scraps of discarded wood so that they could catch a glimpse of those joyous smiles on the third day of the festival.

He would do what he could. Rising from his table, took one of the gladii off the wall and hung it over his shoulder, then put on his thin, worn grey cloak, and put the lists in the leather scrip at his waist.

As he came out of the tablinum into the atrium, Ida approached with a small clay cup, her eyes casting a wary glance at Catus' room.

"A little broth to keep you warm outside," she said.

"Thank you, Ida," Giles replied, and the woman looked up at him, the hint of a smile, the kind that was full of grace and gratitude.

Ida nodded and took back the cup when he had drained it.

"Fortuna be with you today," she whispered.

He nodded. "Stay clear of him as much as you can," Giles said, his voice a whisper. "He's even more hateful this time of year, and I don't think it's because Krelis died this day." He glanced at the floor to his left, where he had found Krelis' body, seven years before. "It's always about money."

"Go easy on them, if you can," Ida said.

"I always do," he replied. "I'll see you later."

Giles went to the door and opened it, expecting to find a line of clients waiting to see Catus, but instead he found the street empty.

Even those who needed something from Catus avoided coming to him during Saturnalia, for they did not wish to ruin what was, to them, the most exciting festival of the Roman calendar.

"Giles Amadea!" came a happy voice as he was about to close the door.

Giles looked up and saw the beaming face of Julian

Corbin, Catus' nephew.

"Salve, Julian Corbin!" Giles said accepting the hand that reached out and grasped his tightly in friendship. Julian already wore the synthesis and pileus, the colourful clothes and felt cap of Saturnalia.

"I see you are ready to celebrate!" Giles smiled.

"As ever, I am full of cheer!" Julian said. "How are you? Your family is well, I hope?"

"Well enough, sir, thank you."

"Please, Giles. You know my name. I'm not your employer. I hope you consider me a friend, and friends use each other's names."

"Julian, then. Yes, thank you. My family is doing well."

"And young Paulus?"

Giles' smile faded slightly, and Julian put his hand on his shoulder.

"Forgive me. I didn't mean to pry."

"Not at all," Giles said, gathering his emotions at the thought of his youngest son. "Alas, the Gods still challenge his health, but I am hopeful that he will be the stronger for it."

"Let me send you a medicus to see him," Julian offered. "He is a friend who owes me a favour. He was a student of Galen's in Alexandria, so he is quite skilled."

"I couldn't. I mean-"

"Don't be silly. You must do all you can to help him, even if it means accepting help from a friend."

"I thank you, Julian."

"Think nothing of it. Young Paulus is the most beautiful and kindly child I've ever had the privilege to meet."

"The Gods smile on you, Julian."

"And may they bless you, your good wife and children, Giles."

It was always a joy for Giles to cross paths with Julian, for no one was more honest and forthright as he. So much more the shock that he was related by blood to the man within the domus behind them.

"How is my uncle's mood this fine day?" Julian asked, his eyebrows raised.

Giles glanced at the door and leaned in close. "It is the time of Saturnalia. He is at his worst."

"I thought as much. Well, wish me luck."

"Tyche guide you, Julian. Now, I must be going about my work." Giles took his hand one more time, turned and walked away down the street.

Julian's smile faded, knowing full well what that meant. Then he turned and went into the atrium of the home, gently closing the door behind him.

"Io Saturnalia!" Julian cried out as he entered the atrium of Catus' domus and made for the door of his uncle's tablinum.

His uncle remained hunched over several piles of denarii and sestercii which he had been counting out by the light of a single clay lamp. He did not look up.

Still smiling, beaming in fact like Sol Invictus, Julian persisted.

"I said, Io Saturnalia!"

The chatter of moving coins stopped and Catus slowly looked up at his nephew with rheumy eyes.

"The Dead to dine on Saturnalia…" he growled.

"Gods forbid, Uncle!" Julian gasped, making the sign against ill-omen. "Surely you don't mean that."

"I do!" Catus snapped, slamming his fist on the table and scattering the piles of coins. This enraged him even more than the jolly air his nephew had brought into his office. His bald head began to go crimson and it seemed that before Julian's eyes, every angry crack and crevice in his uncle's face darkened and deepened. That rictus-of-a-face stared up at Julian, accusing and disgusted. "Why are you so happy all the time when you are poor?"

Julian laughed. "Why are you so dreadful and angry when you are richer than Crassus and Croesus combined?"

Catus shook his head at the ridiculousness of his nephew's statement. Of course the boy did not know that when one had money, the world was always trying to take it from you.

"What good is Saturnalia when people use it to fall deeper into debt, when they honour gods they don't give a bronze as for the rest of the year? They go and buy sigillaria and cerei, food and wine they cannot afford when they should be paying off their debts to people like me. Rather than putting on masks to hide from their responsibilities, or gambling away their money in the streets, they should be working harder at all hours to free themselves of the debt of their lives. No. You celebrate and degrade yourself how you wish at Saturnalia, but let me celebrate it in my own way."

"Celebrate? But you don't celebrate!" This was the first time that Julian's smile faded and the colour rushed to his cheeks such that his visage was filled with such passion and youth that it angered Catus to the point of eruption.

Catus stood up, his arched back stretching to its limit as he faced his nephew on the other side of the table.

"Nephew, listen carefully… If I could have my way in this world, every whoreson who goes about with *Io Saturnalia!* dribbling from his lips would be sent to the darkest, deepest depths of Tartarus to scrimp and scramble in the dark mire of eternity. There and then let them celebrate their utter stupidity in life and see how much good Saturnalia has done them!"

Catus stood breathing like a fighter after a bout, staring up at his nephew, the black hair and bright eyes that were his sister's.

Julian took a deep breath and placed his hands on his uncle's bony shoulders.

Catus let them linger there a moment, but then pushed his nephew's arms away as if the attempted affection were more annoying than the malaria-ridden

Pontine mosquitoes.

Julian was undeterred as Catus went back around to the other side of his table.

"Why do you hate me so, Uncle? The Gods know I have never asked you for anything. I have never berated you for the atrocious treatment of your man, Giles Amadea, nor of the hideous way in which you treat your servant. It is not my place, I know."

"No! It is not your place, so do not begin now!" Catus spat back.

"And it is true that I find myself short of coin every Saturnalia, and I am happy to cry the words *Io Saturnalia!* far and wide along with citizen and slave. Would you have me join the rest of the world in Tartarus? If that is what you wish, Uncle, then you would be very lonely indeed upon this earth."

Julian felt his lip begin to tremble for the great emotion that welled up in him but, determined as ever, and strengthened by the purity of the season, he held fast.

"I say, the Gods bless this season and all that goes along with it. They know my heart and intent are as pure as Vesta's light in this, Uncle. Can the same be said of your own heart and life?"

"Get out of my domus now."

"I'm not finished. The main reason for my coming here was to invite you to a banquet at our home on the Caelian Hill tomorrow. As ever, I reserve the lectus medius for you."

Catus actually laughed, but not in an amused manner. Rather, it was the sort of laugh that darkened the room, if such was possible in that place.

"A banquet? I think not!" He pointed his stylus at Julian. "Why did you ever marry that Etrurian woman? She brought nothing to the marriage, not even lands."

"Because I fell in love with her, Uncle."

Now Catus' eyes blazed. "Love... Love! Then you are an even bigger fool than I already believed you to be. You go back to your sad domus on the Caelian Hill now, Nephew, and leave me be. I'm finished with you."

"I'm sorry if I have angered you, Uncle, but my invitation still stands. I hope you will find it in your heart to join us."

"Be gone now!" Catus shouted.

"I am. Io Saturnalia! And may the blessings of Janus guide you into the new year."

Julian turned and went out into the atrium where he stopped to speak with Ida as she opened the door.

"The Dead to dine on Saturnalia!" Catus shouted one last time.

Julian saw Ida's hands begin to shake as the words exploded from her master's tablinum, and he took them in his and looked into the slave's eyes.

"Do not fear, Ida. There is good in the world beyond these walls," he whispered. Then he reached into the scrip that hung over his colourful synthesis and produced a small linen bundle and handed it to the slave. "Honey cakes from the Forum. Something sweet for you to have tomorrow."

Ida's eyes filled with tears as she hesitantly accepted the bundle, beautifully tied with a sprig of holly and a red ribbon. More than that, however, was the feeling of kindness that the touch of his warm hands gave her. Something of hope.

"May the Gods bless you, sir," Ida said.

"May they bless us all." Julian smiled, opened the door and went out, almost bumping into two men who had been standing on the front stoop, rallying their courage to knock.

"Salve, citizens!" Julian said. "Io Saturnalia!"

The two men smiled wide at the young, bright man. They had not expected such a welcome at this particular domus.

"Io Saturnalia!" they replied together, wearing identical smiles and identical blue tunics, neatly pressed and clean, but not overly ostentatious. "Are you Catus Pompilius?" they asked Julian, quite hopeful now.

"Ah. No, I am not. He is within."

"Is he receiving clients this time of day?" they asked.

"He is, but I would not expect a warm welcome," Julian said. "But do not let me deter you. First tablinum on the right. Ida will show you the way." He smiled one more time at the slave and went down the cobbled street toward the Suburra, praising loudly the work of the slaves at every house as they hung garlands of holly and ivy and other greens over the doors of each domus.

"What a pleasant fellow!" the one man exclaimed to the other as they followed Ida.

She stood beside the door to Catus' tablinum, the linen bundle carefully hidden behind her back as she bowed and the two men moved past her. Once they entered the room, she rushed off to hide the gift.

"Salve, Catus Pompilius!" the men said in concert,

eyes beaming, cheeks red with joy and the effort of climbing the line of the Esquiline.

"What do you want?" Catus said, looking up slowly from his rolls of accounts and evictions.

"Erm," the first man cleared his throat and began. "I am Castor and this is my brother, Pollux. We are here to speak with you and your partner, Krelis Manvilio, to discuss a contribution from you to the Suburan feast to be given on the day of the Sigillaria on December nineteenth."

The second man spoke now. "As you and your partner-"

"Krelis Manvilio has been dead these seven years ago today!" Catus barked. "Now out with it so that you can leave me to my work!"

"Of course, sir," Pollux continued, "as the landlord of most of the tenements in the Suburra, you will be aware of the hardships facing the families who live there. It is crowded, prone to fire, and often ridden with disease."

Castor went on. "Much of the hardships of these poorer citizens of Rome would be lessened with a banquet and small sigillaria for the children, those who are the future of the Empire."

"How much would you like to contribute to this noble cause, Catus Pompilius?" Pollux asked.

"Nothing."

"Ah…if you prefer, sir, we can keep your contribution anonymous, if you do not wish for others to know of your generosity. We know your name is well-respected," Castor almost choked on these last words, but pulled it off.

"I said nothing!" Catus snapped, then leaned back in his hard wooden chair. "Tell me… If things are so bad in the Suburra, why does the Senate not do something about it?" He leaned forward not giving the men a chance to speak further. "And the public banquet in the Forum? Has it been cancelled this year?"

The two men shook their heads.

"If the rats in the Suburra are so hard-done by the world, then there must be other ways in which they can pay their debts, no? Has the Ludus Magnus and other gladiatorial schools stopped accepting men who wish to pay off their debts on the arena sands?"

"No, sir," the men said.

"Have the mines in Sicilia closed for good?"

"No, sir. Sadly not."

"And Rome's ships that ply the Middle Sea, have they all run aground making the need for galley slaves superfluous?"

"No, sir," the men replied, now fully aware of the man, if he could be called such, before them.

"That is good," Catus nodded and seemed to calm down. "For a moment there, I was worried that our great Emperor Severus had lost his wits. You see, gentlemen, I curse this festival day of Saturnalia and any other festival that drives men to madness, waste and frivolity. I am taxed by the emperor enough for his war, let alone for the upkeep of mines, the fleet, and public games that are the disgrace of Rome's calendar. If the people of the Suburra cannot feed themselves, let their fathers step onto the sands, or into the mines and galleys to pay off their debts."

Pollux, whose face was red, spoke now with contempt for the little man before them. "I think I can safely say that the Gods themselves would not wish it so, and that most of the good people of the Suburra would rather die than take the roads you recommend."

"If they would rather die, then so much the better for me!" Catus yelled. "The Suburra would be a less pestilent place, and I could sell those tenements for a fortune!"

Silence hung in the air as Catus stared at the two men whose courage and Saturnalian joy had been sapped by this encounter with so heinous a creature.

"Good day to you both," Catus said, his voice calm as he rounded his desk and sat back down to work.

Without another word, Castor and Pollux left.

When the door slammed shut, Catus grumbled.

"The Dead to dine on Saturnalia…"

The rest of Catus Pompilius' day was taken up with intimidation. He made his way, like a wraith, or reaper of good humour, through the imperial fora, the Aventine and Caelian hills and other places as the shadows lengthened. His grim circuit led him finally to the Suburra where most of his collections originated.

Catus visited a butcher who was busy preparing suckling pigs for upcoming feasts, then a wood carver who was busily making figurines for sale during Saturnalia. Another smoothed and polished sets of knucklebones which he had obtained from the butcher beside after his sheep had been slaughtered. The dark shadow of Catus appeared at the doorways of countless homes in the tenements he owned, demanding the rents owed and threatening the families who were unable to pay the full amount plus the interest they had incurred.

In one most extreme circumstance, when the paterfamilias of one rather large family took it upon himself to threaten Catus, the heartless man even offered to take some of their children away to the slave market as a means of repayment.

For those whose rickety thresholds were darkened by Catus, the sweet joy of Saturnalia turned bitter in their mouths even before it had begun, and it was all they could do to muster a smile or sing a song. Wherever the landlord Catus went, he left discord, fear and argument in place of jollity, hope, and love. He was, this mortal man, a poison among citizen and slave alike.

Not so his man, Giles, who had rushed ahead of his employer, knowing full-well that he would not be left to the collections on his own.

Despite the task pressed upon him, Giles Amadea went about his work with compassion and care, pressing only when he knew the debtors to be lying full to his face. He dealt honestly and evenly with all, accepting what little they could offer and promising to buy them some more time if possible, which it rarely was. Others, he told plainly that if they did not offer him even a small portion of the rent they owed, he would be forced to come back with Catus at the latter's request, and visit harm upon them. It would not happen so long as he steered clear of his employer whom he knew to be stalking the streets at the same time.

But it did happen, that meeting of the two, at one of the crossroad fountains where Catus surprised Giles from behind, pulling tightly on his tunic.

"There you are! Follow me," Catus growled.

Giles followed solemnly, like a mourner, as they went down one of the narrower lanes to a small broken door hanging on rusty hinges.

Inside they found three Syrians, a brother and two sisters, who had been renting the basement of the tenement from Catus since they arrived in Rome in the wake of Emperor Severus' Parthian war. They had not paid their rent in three months, always managing to evade their landlord or his collector.

But now, they had been caught unawares and the three siblings looked up at the grim faces of Catus and his man where they stood at the top of the stairs looking down on their table, set with candles, salads, fresh bread, and steaming meat.

"So…too poor to pay your rents, and yet you dine like eastern kings in the bowels of my basement!"

Catus spat at the table.

The young man stood up abruptly, his right hand, Giles noted, resting on the hilt of a small blade that was on the table top.

The sisters looked nervously at each other and then to their brother as Catus made his way down the stairs.

"Pay now, in full, or you are out in the street," Catus said, his voice gravelly and aggressive.

"We do not have it," one of the sisters pleaded.

"Obviously you do," Catus pointed at the table. "Break his hands," Catus said to Giles over his shoulder.

"Sir?" The former gladiator could sense the danger in the air, and knew that the brother would not give up without a fight. He stepped in front of Catus, aware of the hand gripping slowly about the handle of the knife. "Perhaps you will have the full amount tomorrow?" Giles asked the girls, his eyes glancing at the brother.

"Pay now, or you are out in the street this very night!" Catus yelled.

The brother lunged for the landlord, his blade out, but Giles' arm struck out, deflecting the young man's thrust, his other hand fastening about his wrist so that the blade fell to the ground.

"Not a wise move!" Giles said, as he knocked the lad back onto the table, the sisters screaming in alarm. He didn't feel the cudgel being lifted from his belt soon enough and before he knew it, Catus' arm had swung and struck the brother on the right hand with an audible crunch.

Catus lifted his arm again and struck the young man's face so that two teeth bolted from behind his bleeding lips.

Giles grabbed the cudgel and held his employer fast. "Sir! We'll evict them! Stop!"

Catus rounded on him, his breathing ragged and enraged. "You don't give the orders here!"

"I know that, sir," Giles answered, still holding the cudgel out at the wailing brother. "But it is an ill-omen to kill during Saturnalia. The Gods will curse you for it."

"The Dead to dine on Saturnalia!" Catus spat at the wreck of the festive table. "They deserve to die."

"I'll evict them now, sir," Giles said, his voice deep and even. "Return home with the rents and I'll be along shortly." Giles then handed Catus the leather satchel he had about his shoulder with the monies he had managed to collect, each pouch with a slip of paper indicating the tenant.

Catus weighed the satchel and his frown increased ten-fold. "Do not go home yet. You and I will have a serious discussion when you return." He looked once more at the brother and sisters. "Leave tonight, or I swear you won't see the end of this accursed festival." Then, gripping the satchel from Giles, as well as his own, Catus Pompilius walked slowly up the stairs and back into the darkening street.

Giles turned to the three before him, the cudgel hanging by his side now.

"Pack your things and leave...now."

"We've nowhere to go," one sister pleaded.

"He is evil!" the brother spat, blood dripping onto his chest.

"Yes, he is. But you tried to murder him too." He turned to the brother. "You're lucky only to be evicted." Giles reached into the folds of his tunic, pulled out a small leather pouch, and tossed it to the brother. "This is all I have right now. Take it and leave."

The brother and sisters looked up at the ex-gladiator, confusion and gratitude mingling on their features. Then, quickly, they gathered the few belongings they had from the beds in the corner, a small rough statue of Baal, and what food was not ruined by the scuffle.

Giles waited for them to leave, and when they had gone weeping into the night, he snuffed out the lamp and barred the door from the outside. He did indeed have more names to visit on his list that night, but he had lost the stomach for it.

Besides, he had a meeting with Catus, and that was never a cause for optimism.

The Esquiline Hill was alight with laughter and torchlight as Giles walked up the road that veered from the Suburra's darkness to the treed heights of one of Rome's richer neighbourhoods. He passed early revellers who smiled and danced about him good-naturedly, singing as they skipped away to the tabernae scattered throughout the city.

Normally, Giles would have joined them in their song, perhaps even skipped a step or two, but he did in fact dread the meeting ahead of him. He knew he had gone too far with Catus Pompilius, but he could not stand by and allow the man to kill the brother for a few coins over a place that was not fit for a cache of wine amphora, let alone a family of three.

He thought of his family then. He had risked all on the sands of the Colosseum to win his freedom. *So much blood...* he remembered. *I've had enough for a lifetime.* He looked down at his strong hands as he came onto Catus' street and was disgusted to find spattered blood there on the eve of one of Rome's most sacred festivals!

The street was lit with brightly burning braziers, the polished bronze of their legs decorated with holly and ivy, and the door slaves standing by to welcome various guests for the banquets the wealthy gave in advance of the real celebrations. Litters were already parked along the curb of the stone-cobbled street, their canopies of deep blues and reds also bedecked with greenery, heady perfumes wafting out into the night from their plush interiors.

It seemed the entire Esquiline was in a flurry of final preparations, each domus bursting to let out a titanic 'Io!' to begin the festivities in earnest.

All except one.

Ahead of Giles as he walked, there appeared a dark stretch of street devoid of light and joy, absent song and colour. The wall along the street turned dark and grey, peeling as it poured toward the dark door where the domus of Catus Pompilius squatted like a grotesque barnacle on the body of a lithe sea nymph.

Giles searched the loop of his cingulum for the key and inserted it into the door.

The atrium was dark, lit only by the faint glow of lamplight from Catus' tablinum to the right.

Giles turned to close the front door and was startled by the form of Ida cowering in the shadows. Her lip trembled slightly and there was a faint slickness on the side of her mouth. He stepped toward her, his hand out, but she shook her head, not wanting the contact, but as he took her shaking hand, she leaned against his bulk, her body wracked by silent sobs.

The wall of her servitude down, for only a moment, she looked up, her bleeding lip taught, her eyes pleading for no more kindness, for it was far too painful a thing to experience.

"Dominus is waiting for you," she said, her eyes darting to the doorway before her form faded into the darkness of the sad peristylium beyond.

Giles watched her go and then went into the tablinum.

"Are the Syrians out?" Catus said.

"Yes, sir. They are, and the door is barred."

Catus was silent as he made a mark on one of the wax tablets before him.

"You should not have interfered."

The silence was thick, like coagulating blood, and in that harsh silence, beyond the ringing in Giles' ears, a ringing he had always experienced before confrontation, he saw his family's faces.

"I sought only to keep you from harm, sir," Giles said.

"Oh, I see... You interfered to help me, is that it? Because you were worried for me?" The sarcasm dripped from Catus' mouth like saliva from a slavering wolf. "Do you remember where you were before I hired you?"

"Yes, sir." Giles remembered all too well the days when, newly free of the bonds of being a gladiator, he had been newly married with a baby, and their home a squalid lean-to in a stinking alleyway. Those were days when he had slept but little so that he could stand guard over his wife and child through the long, criminal nights. A time when he had got scraps of food for them by doing the odd job of moving heavy items, unloading cargo at the docks for a bronze as, or other duties slaves with a coin were willing to shirk.

Giles had never stolen a single coin in the days of desperation, no matter how many opportunities had presented themselves.

One day, walking along the rim of the Caelian hill, he had come across a scuffle between two old men and a group of thugs from one of the Caelian collegia. Death had been in the air that day and, still able to taste the blood of the amphitheatre in his mouth, Giles had waded in to prevent the violence. He had beat back five of the aggressors, the remaining three having run for it.

It was only after the encounter that he learned of the two old men he had saved - Catus Pompilius and Krelis Manvilio.

A few days later, Catus, shaken by the encounter, though not admitting as much, sought out the ex-gladiator and offered him a position as a collector of rents. The position paid little, but it did come with the chance to live on the ground floor of one of the tenements owned by the pair of landlords.

The thought of his wife and baby, with another on the way, living in that stinking alleyway was enough to make him accept the work, even from such as Catus.

Now, as Giles stood in Catus' tablinum, staring

down at his pale, bald head, he remembered where he had been.

"I remember," Giles said when Catus did not speak again.

"Good. For I am guessing that you do not wish to go back to your filthy alleyway, this time with five children?"

"No, sir," Giles said, his arms crossed as Catus looked up at him for the first time.

"Nor, I'm guessing, do you want to go back to the arenas for the self-enslavement that so many debtors pursue?"

"Never."

Catus' eyes seemed to glow with a ferocity then. As he felt the power he had over this younger, stronger man grow, he felt stronger himself.

"Then you would do well to remember that, even though you are not my legal slave, I own you Giles Amadea! Without me, you would be nothing and your family would starve."

No they wouldn't! Giles screamed inside. *I would find a way. You do not own me!*

"If you ever countermand me again, or get in the way of my inflicting just punishment on those who seek to cheat me, you and your entire family will find yourselves evicted and back on the streets of this stinking city!" Catus slammed his fist on the table so that his stylus flipped once over and rolled away onto the floor.

Giles bent to pick it up and placed it on the papyrus rolls with lists of names crossed out. "I understand," he said.

"Good," Catus said, bending over his lists one more time, frowning as the sounds of revelry outside began in earnest and sneaked into that dark room. "Now, I know you've not collected all that you were supposed to, so I expect you to go back to it now."

"But, sir, it is almost midnight."

"Did you not hear me?" Catus looked up again, his hoary, wrinkled features daring Giles to gainsay him once more.

"Yes, sir. I'll get right to it."

"Good. I may not be permitted to make you work for the first three days of this accursed festival, but by Death, I'll squeeze every drop of sweat out of you before this day ends. Now go, and in three days, I want you here before the first hour of daylight to start back to work. Do you understand?"

"Yes, sir." Giles nodded and turned to go, willing his mind to think of the joys of the festival that would begin in just a short while. He took a deep breath at the door of the tablinum and turned back to Catus.

"I'll make the collections, sir, do not worry. I always do."

"Get out of here!" Catus mumbled.

"Io Saturnalia," Giles said with a little less gusto than was usual.

"Get out, Gods damn you!"

At the front door of the domus, Ida was waiting for Giles.

"Gods bless you, Ida," he said, his hand on her bony shoulder. He hated to leave her there in that house of misery, especially when most other slaves in the city would be relieved of duties and permitted no small measure of celebration for the next three days. He knew Ida would receive no respite or sigillaria, no chance to feast or light candles.

"Go now, to your family," she said. "Enjoy the days for us both." Tears rimmed Ida's eyes for a moment, but she blinked them away as she opened the door and let Giles out.

As Giles walked away to finish his work, he looked back to see her form gazing out from the shadowed door toward the laughing slaves down the street, before she closed it and slid the bolt home.

Catus hunched over his scrolls and piles of coins for a good while longer, smiling only at a complete stack or fully-checked list of names successfully evicted.

Oh, to find joy in such things was something that even the cruelest of Gods must find fault in. Nothing noble in it, to be sure, but such was not Catus' thinking.

He ran his finger down the list of names continuously, counted coin without end. He was nearly finished summing a particularly large portion of the accounts when the peal of laughter and song tore at his ears from the street outside.

"The Dead to dine on Saturnalia!" he cursed, reaching for one of the cudgels he had taken from Giles' tablinum across the way. "I'll knock the song from their mouths!" he said as he stormed to the front door of his domus, threw it open, and raged into the street.

There, in the dark patch of street before him, Catus lunged, as quick as his old corpse would allow, at a group of young Equestrians who were drinking and dancing there.

"Whoa! Easy, old man!" one of them said, pushing his friend out of the cudgel's swing as Catus brought it around toward his head.

"He's mad!" another yelled.

"To Hades with all of you! Shut your mouths and be gone!" He swung again, taking one of them on the shoulder and extorting a yelp.

The first young man moved in quick-as-a-cat and pushed Catus so that he stumbled and fell onto the ground before his front door, his head glancing off one of the paving slabs.

The young man's friends grabbed him and pulled him away.

"He's not worth it!" another said, and they began to walk on as Catus mumbled curses at their backs, trying to get himself up.

"Io Saturnalia!" they called back, carrying on with their song and quite forgetting the encounter with the aged Catus behind them.

It seemed a few minutes at least that Catus lay there, anger boiling inside of him. He was vaguely aware of several people walking around him, but none offering help as he lay prostrate. Not that he would have accepted aid. No. He would have heaped his vitriol upon them.

Eventually he rose and stared bleary-eyed and full of hate down the street in both directions, cursing at every shout of 'Io!' that reached his ears.

"The Dead to dine on Saturnalia!" he shouted, and he had never meant it more than at that very moment. He would have seen each one of them dead if he could.

Catus then turned upon the stone to make his way back to his door.

He had gone only three steps before his feet rooted themselves to the ground and his blood ran icy cold, for his own black door now glowed with an icy light. The light did not come from the thick oak panels, nor the iron rivets that studded the entirety of its surface, nor the keyhole or handle. The ethereal light that burned slowly and surely, like a fog bank with a light in its belly, came from the ancient gorgon-headed knocker set in the surface of the door.

Catus tried to get his breathing as best he could, his eyes darting to either side down the street to see if anyone else spied what he did in that moment, but it seemed that this once, no one was around. He bent down to pick up the cudgel he had dropped and approached the door.

The gorgon head stared straight ahead, its eyes vacant and still, even as the serpents of its hair writhed and hissed, many of them stretching out to Catus' own face with fangs and forked tongues.

Hisssssssss...

Catus swept the cudgel up, but the snakes avoided it with ease, darting for his face once more.

"Ida!" Catus shouted, but the slave was away sleeping in her tiny cell-of-a-cubiculum. "Ida! Wake up!" he shouted again, but this time, instead of waking his slave, he roused the gorgon!

Upon the door, the gorgon head frowned in its serpentine frame and then the eyes closed and opened again, but slowly, to reveal a face, the face of Krelis!

It stared straight at the mortal man before it, those vacant eyes now filled with such fierce light that it would look deep into the man before it and wrench the heart from within his chest.

Catussssssssss the gorgon hissed.

"Ahhh!" Catus screamed as he stumbled back and fell once more upon the hard stone cobbles with his eyes shut as if he feared turning to stone from that ghostly gaze.

Silence fell on that dark part of the street once more and after a moment, Catus dared a look.

The door was black and silent once more.

Catus rose more quickly this time and made for the door, his steps pausing just before it where he hit the knocker with his cudgel, extracting only a solid thud from it. He shook his head and spat, convincing himself that the attack by the Syrian brother had unnerved him more than he wanted to admit. With that thought, he promised himself violent retribution upon the man should he ever see him in the city again.

He opened the door and slammed it shut behind him, ensuring the bolt was well locked in its iron home. He then stared at the back of the door, his gnarled fingers going over the surface.

Nothing there.

Clutching the cudgel, Catus went into his tablinum to extinguish the lamp that he had left burning, cursing himself for the waste of oil. He covered the coins he had been laying out, and then took another key and locked the door of his tablinum, which was as solid as his front entrance.

The domus was dark as he made his way out of the atrium, through the garden, and up the stairs leading to the second level. He paused to look down at the garden, which one could not really call a garden, so black and lifeless was it. Dry leaves skittered around it as a cold wind picked its way inside, weaving around the columns of the peristylium.

Leaning on the crumbling marble railing, Catus saw a brief glow on the far side of the garden, and then a milky-lighted shape of a man pass from behind one column to the next. He watched a second more for the light to pass between the next set of columns but it did not come. However on the wind, there was a sound of wailing, muffled and sad, as of mourners at a funeral in the streets.

Catus turned quickly and made his way up the stairs and down the short hallway to his cubiculum at the back of the domus. He immediately closed the door and slid the bolts home, one at the top and one at the bottom.

His room was dark but for the single oil lamp Ida had lit before taking to her mat in the kitchen far below.

"Curse her," he grumbled. "What a waste."

Catus walked past the shelves where he kept boxes of coin, and more dusty scrolls. The walls were bare but for a single, faded layer of red paint that had long faded to the colour of a rotted pomegranate. He searched the room, not admitting to himself how shaken he was by what had happened at the door in the street, or what he had just seen in the very garden below him. He felt his guts with his bony hand and cursed the cheese he had eaten earlier.

He paused to gaze out of the window at the back of his cubiculum to see the warm glow of lights scattered all about the city as candles, lamps and braziers were lit everywhere.

"Such a waste!" he muttered.

Catus turned back to his dark room and the sole couch in its midst where he lay himself down, blowing out the oil lamp on the table beside. He didn't bother to undress, for he could start his work all the earlier next day.

He had closed his eyes but a moment when a shuffling reached his ears from outside his cubiculum door. The steps were similar to those of a lazy slave, reluctant to carry on with the drudgery that was their lot.

"I'm trying to sleep, Ida!" Catus said loudly. "Be quiet or be gone to the mines!" He spoke loudly, boldly, but some small part of his fierce disposition ran cold once more, a sliver of fear running deep as an ethereal light seemed to grow more and more intense at the bottom of his door frame.

"Who's there?" he demanded, his voice tremulous, his hand reaching for the cudgel which he had laid upon the floor beside his couch.

Before Catus' very eyes, the bolt at the top slid open, and then the second at the bottom of the door.

"What is this?" Catus said beneath his breath.

But before he could find some thought of reason to explain the situation in which he found himself, a ghostly hand pushed through the door, leading the way for a togate apparition.

Catus gripped the cudgel and jumped to his feet, ready for whatever action might be required, but the moment he gazed upon the face before him, he froze, the weapon dropping with a deafening echo upon the marble floor.

The shade before him was none other than Krelis Manvilio!

Catus stood there, his brow sweating, though he felt

colder than he had ever done before. He tried to speak but all he could do was stare at the pale apparition whom he recognized as his former business partner. He shook his head and shut his eyes, hoping the shade would disappear upon opening them, but it was not to be.

It was Krelis Manvilio who stood there, staring at him, the sickly light that emanated from him filling the room more than any lamp or brazier.

Catus shivered but found his tongue.

"What do you want?" he said, his eyes noting the crack in the shade's skull where ghostly blood had bubbled and dried, staining the toga's shoulder.

"Much!" the shade said, not smiling, not frowning, but gazing directly at the mortal man before it.

"Who, or what, are you?" Catus demanded.

The shade did not speak immediately, but moved closer until it was but a few feet away. As it came closer, there was a muted screeching and hissing at the door.

Catus dared to gaze beyond the shade to see what it was and he spied three winged women, their faces distorted and fanged, their hair hanging like rotten weeds about their shoulders.

"Do not look to the furies at my back, for they are my own doom and go with me evermore," the shade said, its head turning to catch Catus' eye. "Look to me, for what I have to say concerns you greatly, Catus Pompilius."

Catus stepped back, the shade too close for his own comfort. "You have not answered me," he said then. "Who are you?"

The shade smiled, though the act was completely devoid of mirth.

"You know in that black heart who I was." It pointed at Catus, a pale, rotting and broken hand. "As to what I am now... I am despair and grief... I am regret and pain... I am sorrow and damnation..."

The shade frowned then, and Catus thought that it would weep if it could.

"In the world of men, you knew me as Krelis Manvilio. Together you and I worked at bringing misery upon the people of Rome."

"It was business," Catus said. "It still is!" He rubbed his eyes and shook his head.

"You do not believe what your eyes tell you," the shade of Krelis said. "Nor the cold you feel in the depths of your body at this moment."

"No, I do not!" Catus said.

"Why do you doubt that I am before you?"

"Because I have been hounded by those seeking to cheat me, to harm me. My senses have been numbed by a block of rotten cheese that was given me." Catus gripped his guts, mistaking the fear he felt for a riot of indigestion.

The shade came closer to Catus, those terrible, pained eyes directly before his own, and a sudden stench of death in the air.

"Nevertheless…I *am* here, Catus Pompilius, and you would do well to hear me now."

"I don't need you. Leave me be!" Catus pleaded.

"I will not, for I am here not for myself…it is too late for me… I am here for you and your own salvation."

The furies behind the shade had come into the room now and were slavering at Krelis' back, their clawed hands raking at him, hissing, hurrying him on. The shade actually winced.

"My time is short," the shade said, and in its eyes there was a memory of the man that Catus had once known very well indeed.

"Wha...what...is it?" Catus stuttered.

"I am here to warn you, Catus Pompilius. When my mortal form died, you became more a man of business than ever you were -"

"You always were good at it, Krelis," Catus interjected. "But your death left me with the weight of our business upon my shoulders!" He actually pointed at the spectre.

Krelis' shade shook its head and laughed, a cold humourless laugh that threatened to sap any remnant of courage Catus thought he might have had in that moment.

"You enjoyed the *business* of making people suffer. You were thrilled that I fell to my death."

"You were always better at it than I was, but I brought this city to heel!"

"And it will be your doom, Catus Pompilius," Krelis said, his pale face sad now. "Unless you harken to the one chance of hope I have been told to offer you now."

"Hope? What hope can a dead man offer me?" Catus crossed his arms, his chin sticking out but then shrinking as the furies looked momentarily at him.

"A single thread, a light in the labyrinth of dark eternity in which I am now cursed to dwell evermore. A chance to avoid these…"

At this the furies writhed and danced and clawed his back and his ghostly toga shredded and stained with blood.

"Krelis!" Catus stepped forward but the shade held up a hand.

"Listen now! You will be visited by three immortals."

"Immortals?" Catus' blood froze even more, but his doubts already began to creep in and poison the seed of optimism and belief that Krelis had tried to plant. "I don't think it necessary."

"Expect the first tomorrow at the first hour after midnight."

"Can they not all come at once and have the business done?"

"Expect the second the second hour after midnight." The shade's voice grew fainter and weaker as he moved toward the window of the cubiculum looking over the city.

"Where are you going, Krelis? Stay and give me

comfort."

"I have no more to give, Catus Pompilius. The Gods demand this of you, and if you wish to escape my eternal torture you will-"

At that moment the furies stuck their claws into his back and he cried out, a pitiful, pained cry that echoed as if through time.

Krelis' eyes darted to Catus one last time.

"Expect the third in his own time…"

With those last words, Krelis was lifted into the air and out of the window by the furies.

Catus rushed to the open window to watch Krelis' form being carried off until it disappeared among a chorus of crying and dying, of tortured voices full of regret. He looked out over the city to find the warmth of candle, brazier and lamp had gone out, and the sounds of Rome's dancing and singing had been doused by the darkness. Then a series of violent fires flashed and rose up, kindling even more screams and wailings such as he had never heard.

"Krelis!" Catus yelled out the window, but his voice was drowned out and his eyes filled with fear as he spied the pale lighted forms of people in the streets below pursued by their own furies.

The shades of the dead ran for their eternal, meaningless lives, each from their own personal tormentors whom they could not escape. They tried to run into temples, or the homes of those they had known in life, but the doorways were barred to their shade. They begged and pleaded with those whose lives were upon the filthy streets of Rome, asked them for the chance to help them in their plight, but the mortals were deaf to them, as deaf and indifferent to them as they themselves had been in life.

Catus shook his head and slammed the window shut. He stumbled backward, slipped on the cudgel that lay upon the floor and went down into darkness upon the black marble of his cracked floor.

III

THE FIRST IMMORTAL

Catus woke slowly, rubbing his head where he had bumped it in his fall. He pushed himself up and leaned upon his sleeping couch, his face buried in the lumpy mattress and blankets until his head stopped spinning. Once it did, the memory of what had happened rushed upon him and he whirled around to scan the room, his hand groping for the cudgel.

It was as dark and bare as ever it had been.

"I must have dreamt such a thing," he told himself. "Krelis…you always were a bother. Making more work for me!"

Outside in the streets there were shouts of 'Io!' on top of song and raucous laughter, and Catus shook his head.

"The Dead to dine on Saturnalia…"

Just then he heard the loud crackle of fire very close, and then smelled something. He fumbled for the tinder box on his table and lit the small bronze lamp that sat there. Taking up the lamp, he turned to the door of his cubiculum and saw that a light, softly-lit smoke was snaking its way into his room from beneath the door.

"My money!" he panicked with fear as he fumbled with the bolts on his door, worried that his home was aflame. He threw open the door expecting to find angry orange flames licking up the walls and his slave screaming.

What he did find was his domus intact, but not in its usual state of being. In fact, it was suffused with a warm light that he had never seen before. Colour had crept into the walls and floors, and the myriad mosaic works of art he usually stomped upon glowed very faintly beneath the layers of dust and dirt as if wanting to come to life.

And that smell…so faint and sweet on the air!

Catus inhaled and found himself thinking of sweet wood smouldering gaily in a hearth or brazier. He frowned.

"What is this?" he said as he moved along the marble railing to the stairs and made his way down to the garden. When he reached the bottom, he looked around, the cudgel gripped tightly in his bony hand, and spied a brilliant light emanating from a room at the back of the domus.

It was the lararium, that place which served as the beating heart in most homes, the place where families honoured the gods who watched over them. It glowed so brightly in that moment that it was as if a sun was bursting over the horizon in that very space.

"Impossible," Catus said as he made his way through the dead leaves of his garden toward the room he usually reserved for the storage of brooms and empty containers, the implements of slavery which he never deigned to touch. He had never entered the lararium, never lit a flame there, or uttered a single prayer to god or goddess. It had always been darkened.

But now, oh now, it pulsed with warmth and light, and smelled as sweetly as a spring field in full bloom.

He moved closer to it, ready with his cudgel to batter the intruder, or if it was his slave, to berate her with his wicked tongue. However, when he reached the door frame, he stopped and stared, and the weapons he had been ready to use fell away.

All objects had been cleared from the lararium which was now a proper shrine. The walls were as clean as could be, including the short wall that separated mortals from the Gods and their altars. All was shining and bright.

Catus walked in, clearly a thing out of place, though it was his own domus. At that moment, the light grew so intense that he had to cover his eyes with one hand and grip the short wall with his other for fear of falling again.

Then he felt it…the presence.

It was not cold as had happened earlier in the night, but rather warmer than he could recall ever being. He tried to open his eyes but the light burned them until he fell upon his knees.

"What is this?" he mumbled from the fold of his arm.

"You are unused to my light, Catus Pompilius."

It was a voice of song and of love. A voice of daughter, wife and mother, of care and nurture. The sound made Catus' chest tighten and long for something, but he steeled himself against the feelings that the sound stirred in him, his fear of what he would see when he opened his eyes overcoming him.

"Who are you?" he said from behind his curtained lids.

"Open your eyes, Catus Pompilius. I mean you no harm."

He could not help but obey. Slowly, he raised his head from where he leaned upon the short wall.

There was an altar of pure white marble upon which sat a wide shallow bowl of polished bronze. Inside of the bowl there burned a gently dancing flame atop a lattice of scented wood.

Catus' eyes adjusted to the light and then he saw her, a goddess, sitting upon the broad ledge beyond the flames.

She smiled at him and his hard features softened at once, though his mind spun with questions he demanded answers to.

"Who are you?" Catus observed her closely and noted that the goddess before him was young and beautiful and tall, but that her eyes revealed a kindness and wisdom of ages. There was empathy and understanding there, nurture and love, all of which were as foreign to Catus as the faraway sands of Parthia.

The goddess stood now, tall above the flames which lit her long, pale hair with firelight. Her eyes danced and shone above the flames and she smiled at him.

"You do not know me?"

"I confess I do not," Catus said, his mind set to speaking harshly at first, but as the words came they were softened and respectful.

"I am the flame that burns in every Roman's home, that beats at the heart of this ancient city. My light never goes out once it is kindled."

"You are…Vesta?"

She nodded.

"You are the first immortal to visit me?"

"I am."

He tried to stand then, but found he could not. "I do not know why you might come to me now. I have never offered sacrifice to you."

"Or to any other god or goddess," she confirmed.

"Then perhaps you should leave me to my sleep."

The flame in the bowl dimmed then, and the goddess' features darkened.

"Take heed, Catus Pompilius," she warned. "No mortal who ignores the Gods' grace will have peace in the Afterlife."

Catus was afraid then. "Am…am I to die, then?"

"That is up to you. I am here to kindle some thought, some feeling in you… If you will allow it."

"Pah! I think I would rather sleep."

She ignored him and held out her hand.

"Am I not liable to burn if I take your hand?"

"You can trust in me, Catus Pompilius, though the sentiment be utterly alien to you."

Catus' shaking hand reached out to take Vesta's and the room was filled with blinding white light.

Catus screamed.

They were soaring through the air, and beneath them the Seven Hills of Rome faded away, as did the silvery line of the river Tiber as they sped north, faster than any eagle, night turning to day, the world in all its colour whirling beneath them.

Catus' feet dangled over the abyss, and the rise in his gut made him clench at his stomach with his left hand, the right engaged in gripping the goddess' hand tightly, burning.

The goddess…

Catus dared a look up and to the side to see Vesta, all in brilliant white, her sacred fire flying along before them.

She did not look upon him or acknowledge the shouts of fear that burst from his lips the entire way, the pleadings to return him to his domus. Ever on she led him, soaring along the edge of mountains and green valleys, the sun setting and rising continuously until they began to descend toward a land more beautiful than any other, where the hills and forests surrounded vineyards and villas, where prime spots were given over to the Gods and temples erected. The grey-blue smoke of offerings rose into the air to dance across a landscape that was painted green and white with new-fallen snow.

They set down on the outskirts of a hill-top town in a field where the vines were newly-trimmed, their orderly rows looking onto the valley below in one direction and toward the open city gates in the other.

Catus released the goddess' hand and staggered against one of the posts supporting the vines.

The vine blackened and withered beneath his touch and he jumped back at the result, stumbling in the snow beside the fiery sacred bowl.

"Stand now and walk with me," Vesta commanded,

her voice firm but not altogether unkind. "Do you know this place?" she asked.

Catus stopped and, for the first time, looked around, his senses returning.

"Why…this is the town where I was born and raised!" he exclaimed, wide-eyed and awed. "But how did we come so easily to Etruria from Rome?" He knew he sounded out of sorts, for there had been nothing easy about the journey he had just undertaken. "What could possibly be here for me now?"

"The Past," Vesta said, her eyes gazing upon him from beneath the cowl of her white robes.

"I do not care for the past," he said, crossing his arms. And it was true! Catus Pompilius usually prided himself on his ability to focus on the next payment or deposit, the next financial battle won, or rent collected. He had not thought of his childhood home for some time. "How is it possible?"

"You ask a goddess to explain what your mortal mind cannot comprehend. I have brought you to the Past to remind you of some things you have long forgotten. We may walk unseen and unheard in this place, for these are pale shadows of the life and world that has already gone before. Come," she said, "let us walk."

Vesta set out along the rows of vines toward the town's gate, her sacred fire leading the way before them.

As they went, Catus gazed about him in utter astonishment, for the voices of the past rushed upon him as a bolt of lightning.

The laughter of young boys burst into the wintry air as they charged up the hill from the valley below, each upon a small pony. Vines decorated each of their brows, and each wore colourful clothes of gay patchwork as they charged laughing through the fields, their voices sparkling like a summer stream lit by the sun.

"Hey ho, lads!" Catus suddenly called out. "Titus! Quintus! Silvius!" he called, rushing forward to catch their eyes as they trotted past and along the line of the town walls. He turned to the goddess as she approached the spot where he waited. "Why, I know each and every one of those young boys. They do indeed seem to be enjoying themselves."

Catus' smile faded and his features creased again as they disappeared from sight around the walls and their laughter fell away on the cold, crisp air.

"They cannot hear you, Catus Pompilius," Vesta reminded him.

"Yes...of course," he said. "I had forgotten. But why were they not at their studies, or working in the fields or the town? What reason for the leisure? I remember each of their families being hard workers. Why so lax?"

Vesta looked upon the man before her with sadness and pity, emotions that he recognized and seemed to grow stubborn at.

"It is the first day of Saturnalia," she said. "Even in this remote place, the sacrifice to Saturn was made at the temple at the bottom of the valley." She pointed, and Catus looked to see the smoke wafting up into the air from far below in a place hidden among the trees and fields. Along the road there came a long procession of villagers, citizens and slaves, all happy and singing, carrying lighted cerei of Saturnalia back to their homes before the great public feast to which they all contributed.

Vesta smiled as she watched them all coming. "For three days, they shall not work at all, but celebrate the lives they lead and the gods who watch over them and their bountiful fields. Families shall come together by the sacred light of myriad cerei in homes hung with thick greenery from the land and wine born of the earth. For many it is the brightest time of year."

Catus' face grew sullen and he crossed his arms as the people flowed past him. "A terrible waste of time and denarii," he muttered.

"Do you think so, Catus Pompilius? Look at their faces, the joy written upon them, the lightness in each person's step from the oldest to the youngest. Do you call it waste because you truly believe it, or because your thoughts drift to the only domus in this place where Saturnalia chills the very air you breathe and no sigillaria are exchanged?"

Catus Pompilius remembered now, all too well, that lonesome, dark home of his father's on the far side of the town, the gates usually barred.

Suddenly they were there, within the unplanted peristylium of his childhood home. No fire was lit, and no laughter bounced off of the walls, as is common in places where children dwell.

A great sadness and anger washed over Catus then and he felt himself gravitate a step or two toward the light of Vesta's fire.

But the goddess did not touch him then or give him succour, for he was too lost in the feelings of that place, or lack thereof, to be mindful even of her touch.

Catus' eyes immediately wandered to the faint light

of the tablinum where his father worked away, preparing for his next trip to Massilia where he had business.

"He was always working," Vesta said.

"I can't recall a time when he was not. A hard worker, he was," Catus said sadly.

"A hard man."

"Yes…always…" Catus said, his voice a whisper.

"But he is not the only one in this place, is he?"

Catus shook his head and walked to the far side of the peristylium to stand before a closed door.

Vesta took his hand and pulled him into the small cubiculum.

There, before Catus, was his younger self, hunched over a small, dimly lit table, a stylus clutched tightly in his hand as he went over the accounts and other tasks his father set to test and train him over the days that the scholae were closed.

"My father did not want me wasting time during the dies festus, and so he set me tasks to help train me in account keeping. He inserted deliberate errors to catch me up."

"No child should lead so lonely an existence, should they?"

Catus found he could not speak then as he sat on the bed that was once his, and looked down on the young boy before him. He saw that his young features were hardening even then, and the memories of pain, resentment and loneliness that flooded his stony heart were all too much to bear.

"My father hated me. He always did."

"Why?"

Catus sniffed. "My mother died in childbirth, bringing me into the world. The Gods took her from us."

"And your father punished you for it."

"Yes. Always. This domus never knew warmth or laughter while I was here."

"But you are mistaken, are you not?" Vesta corrected. "There was another member of your family... Your sister?"

"Octavia..." Catus felt his eyes burning and his lip tremble. "Yes..." he closed his eyes and when he opened them, the boy before him aged a few years. "What is this?" Catus looked to the goddess behind him.

"Another Saturnalia in this place," she answered.

The Catus before him was still at work on tasks set by his father, but he did so with more confidence and determination.

The aged Catus stood and looked down on the work, nodding with pride and approval at the way in which the accounts were set, seeing that the deliberate errors set by his father were indeed caught and corrected. He remembered how it felt to catch his father up, to not let him best him. The man had never been happy with his work, and so young Catus had resolved that he should best him in anyway he could.

Then, the door to the cubiculum burst open and in came Octavia Pompilia! Oh, she was a ray of sunshine in that dark place. Newly married to a fine wine merchant of Florentia, her cheeks were rosy with life, her smile enough to lift the spirits of the most sour mortal.

"Catus!" she cried as he whirled around in his chair. "My brother! I've missed you!"

Young Catus sprang to his feet just in time to catch her as she threw herself into his arms, smelling sweetly of clove perfume and the air of outdoors.

"Octavia? What are you doing here?"

"I've just travelled for hours to fetch you, brother! My Marcus has insisted that you come and join us for the entirety of Saturnalia. His business has done extremely well this year and he has taken it upon himself to throw a wonderful banquet for all our friends and family."

"Really?" Young Catus was unbelieving. Could it be possible? "Are you sure father will allow it?"

"How can he not?" she said. "It will cost him nothing, and you know how I have a way of convincing him." She winked and smiled that joyful smile that had always been the sole source of warmth in their home. Octavia had always taken care of Catus since he was born, being four years older than him, and of a supremely caring disposition. She still cared for him.

"You have asked him?" young Catus enquired.

"Not yet. He was busy speaking with a messenger from Rome just as I arrived, so I came to tell you first so that you can gather your things." Octavia looked back out of the open cubiculum door to see the messenger leaving their father's tablinum. "Come! I'll ask him now. You wait outside."

Together, brother and sister ran around the

peristylium until they were before their father's room. Catus stopped, leaning against the wall as she entered.

"Io Saturnalia, Father!" she said as she entered, her voice light and airy.

"Octavia!" their father said, his voice for once happy, for he had not seen her in some weeks. "What brings you here? Is something amiss in Florentia?"

"No, Father. All is perfect. Marcus is as kind as ever, and his business thrives."

"Good. I'm glad to hear it. It was a good match for you and our family." Their father nodded and went to sit back at his work.

At this point, Vesta led Catus into the tablinum to stand beside father and daughter.

Octavia watched her father carry on with his work, and the enthusiasm in her voice turned toward doubt, but she pressed on.

"Father, I've come to invite you and Catus to join us for Saturnalia in Florentia. Marcus and I are throwing a magnificent banquet for all our friends and family and we want you to be there. I shan't take 'No' for an answer!"

"Saturnalia?" her father said. "Surely not. Why

waste time and money on such a thing as that?"

"As the poet said, it is 'the very best of days!'"

"As a woman, you have time for poetry, my dear daughter. But a man of business does not. Nor does he have leisure to waste away for seven days of feasting."

Octavia smiled to herself then, having been ready for some such answer.

"There will be a great many merchants at the banquet, Father. Men with whom you may be able to strike up new partnerships."

The aged Catus smiled at his sister's tact, but his smile faded as the memory returned.

Their father looked up, smiling at his daughter. "Ever the keen mind, my girl. Yes. I will come."

"Really?" she asked.

"Yes. It is a good idea. We have need of more connections. The competition is growing fierce across the Middle Sea. We need to plan ahead." He then turned toward the doorway and shouted. "Catus! Pack your things!"

Young Catus could not contain himself and slid into the tablinum from his spying position outside the door.

"Oh, Father! It won't take me but a moment to pack for Florentia! Thank you! Io Saturnalia!" Catus shouted.

"Quiet down now, Catus!" their father barked. "You will not be joining us in Florentia."

"But, Father?" Octavia burst out. "You just said that you would be joining us?"

"I am, yes. But Catus will be going to Rome."

"Rome?" the young Catus repeated.

"Yes," his father said. "The messenger who just left was from one Salvator Peli in Rome. He has agreed that you may begin as an apprentice with him as soon as possible."

"But Father," Octavia said. "The dies festus is in effect. No business will be done during Saturnalia. Surely Catus can come for three days to Florentia then make his way to Rome?"

"Out of the question. Salvator Peli said the same thing, but I managed to convince him that Catus should start straightaway and get a jump on things. Best not waste time, eh Catus?" He stared at his son with those stony eyes, and the youth withered on the spot.

"Yes, sir…" The young Catus turned and went to

pack his things.

As the scene faded before his eyes, Catus watched the shadow of his sister's lovely face as she stared at their father, a single tear running down her cheek as she turned and went out of the tablinum.

"Your sister loved you very much," Vesta said to Catus.

"She was everything to me..." he said, his voice hoarse and wrung with grief. "I never saw her again after that day."

"She died three years later," the goddess confirmed, her hand upon Catus' shaking shoulder.

"Yes...yes she did."

"But she did leave behind a son, did she not?"

"Yes. She did."

"Your nephew!"

Catus nodded.

"He looks very much like her, in body and the kindness of his spirit."

Catus said nothing as the goddess stared at him, her fire burning fiercely between them and the scene fading away completely.

"Let us visit another time at Saturnalia," she said, and Catus wailed as the earth fell away from them and they were off into the night sky once more...

They landed in the broad space of a warehouse along the banks of the Tiber, the evening water lapping happily outside, but barely audible above the clamour of voices and shouts of 'Io!' that gathered all about.

"I remember this place!" Catus exclaimed. "It's the warehouse of Salvator Peli in Rome where I was an apprentice. And look! There he is!" Catus pointed to the end of the warehouse where a short, dark man was just finishing up some paperwork which he promptly stashed away as his wife Melia came dancing into the space.

"Everybody stop!" Peli shouted. "Io! Io! Io!" He came from around the back of the enormous table where he had been working, clasping his hands and smiling wider than any man might have thought possible. For a moment, he stood gazing at the scene of his business as if in great anticipation of the time to come. He wore a simple but immaculate toga for his daily work, the wool of the highest quality, always pristine white, as clean and neat as his very business.

As Melia approached with a basket of woven ivy crowns, he dashed toward her, kissed her upon the lips and, with a reverence not to be overlooked, took the top-most crown and placed it upon his own head.

Salvator Peli clapped loudly and shouted again. "Io Saturnalia, my busy bees! I command you all to cease your wonderful toils and prepare yourselves and this place for a banquet like no other! The best of days is upon us, and I won't have any of you neglecting your duty to the gods of the season by toiling away. Come now! All of you!"

From the shadows of the warehouse, the goddess Vesta and Catus watched as the entire place was transformed from a warehouse with bolts of cloth, racks of amphorae, and rows of tables where free men and women worked, to a large, bright triclinium. From anterooms, young men carried couches which were laid out with bright cushions in an enormous rectangle, with a large one for Salvator Peli and his wife at the far end.

"There I am!" Catus said, suddenly excited. "Look how young and strong I am!" He stepped forward, the better to see himself as he carried a couch with his then friend, Konstantin Modestus. "That there," he turned to the goddess who smiled upon the brightening scene, "that there was Modestus," Catus said. "He looked up to me so. We were inseparable, we were. Always going about Rome with some of the others, dicing and laughing and…" his voice faded away, stoppered in his throat as a young woman came into the warehouse in the midst of a group of other young ladies.

"Junia…" Catus' voice was a soft breath.

"Salvator Peli's daughter," Vesta added, coming up behind Catus to peer over his shoulder at the young woman who wore a sea blue stola, her long, graceful neck enhanced by a simple golden teardrop necklace which Catus himself had given her.

Catus stood beside his younger self and together they stared at the young woman, the one smiling from cheek to cheek, the other attempting to tear his eyes from the girl before him and all of the memories that came rushing back to him.

She gazed with pure adoration in their direction, her lithesome hand taking the necklace she wore and kissing it as the other girls around her dispersed and took up their places upon the couches with the young men they liked best.

Then the scene absolutely exploded into colour and joy all around the aged Catus, a ghost in their midst whose shadow was far outshone by the light of the goddess behind him. Upon the tables laid out before the sea of couches, great platters of steaming meats and breads were laid beside veritable orchards of fruit and the very best of wines from Peli's own cellars. A deep green corona was set upon the head of every person there, and it was as if such circlets carried magical properties, for they transformed each and every person there present into a celebrant of utmost sincerity.

The food laid out, Peli and Melia themselves went around the gathering with silver jugs to pour wine into the cups of their friends and workers and wish them well.

Catus watched with a rush of remembrance as Junia placed a special crown of ivy and holly which she had fashioned, upon the head of his younger self. Oh! How her eyes danced and sparkled in the light cast by the crackling brazier nearby, and how that forgotten Catus smiled back at her as he slowly kissed her hand, his eyes closing in the act, only to open as Peli himself pat him, his favourite apprentice, upon the shoulder.

"Io Saturnalia, my dears!" the pseudo-father said, his smile so broad it was liable to crack his face in two.

"Io Saturnalia!" the young Catus replied with vigour as he raised a cup to his hosts, the sentiment echoed by the entire gathering.

"Io Saturnalia!" they all cried gleefully, even as a troupe of masked musicians and acrobats bounded into their midst to bedazzle them all even more with Saturnalian spirit.

But that aged ghost of Catus ignored the revels, for he was drawn only to that single couch where his former self clasped hands with that lovely and loving girl beside him. He stood above them as if trying to recall more acutely the now foreign feelings the younger man swam in that night, and the sentiments made him shudder and wail.

"She loved you very much," Vesta said, her motherly hand upon Catus' shoulder.

"And I her," he wept, his tears lost in the hard creases of his care-worn face.

"And her family accepted you into their fold much more than your own father ever did, didn't they?"

"Yes," Catus replied, looking to Salvator Peli and Melia, two joyous and caring Bacchantes if ever there were some.

"But was that night, and every one like it, a disgusting waste?" Vesta suddenly said, her light dimming intentionally.

Catus wheeled on her, his eyes horror-struck.

"Peli's denarii could have been better-spent, could

they not?" she continued. "What a fool he was, to dance and laugh and spend so easily…to waste anything on the rabble that worked for him."

The voices about the gathering grew silent, though they continued to revel all about Catus.

"How can you say such a thing?" he accused. "Look at all the joy he gave us for but a few denarii of his meagre fortune!"

"But the waste must have upset you, no?" Vesta asked.

Catus shook his head, his face confused, the torment behind his eyes making him dizzy.

Vesta's light grew brighter then and she spoke softly as Catus looked back to that couch where he had never been happier. "Come…we will visit another Saturnalia's eve…"

The scene spun and faded, and then Catus and Vesta found themselves in the midst of the Forum Romanum, standing on the steps of the temple of Venus and Rome, facing the mass of the Colosseum.

There, on the steps of the temple of that dread goddess of the heart, stood Catus and Junia, but one year later, their faces unsmiling.

The younger Catus clutched a satchel of accounts and collections and appeared to find it hard to look into the eyes of the young woman before him, her clothes faded now as much as the light in her eyes.

"Can you not help my father this one time, Catus?" she pleaded as she stood before him. "It was not his fault that the shipments were destroyed by the storm."

"I cannot," Catus replied. "I need my own funds to buy up properties. The market is good for it now and, well, your father's business is lost. There is nothing for it." His voice was cold and removed, carrying none of the warmth and love that it formerly knew. He did not even reach out as the flood gates of her lustrous eyes opened up, a sad offering to the Goddess of Love.

"Your father spent too much and did so unwisely, Junia," the young Catus said. "He will have to go to the money lenders. It is the nature of business, and I cannot afford to help him. But I will help you." He tried reaching for her arm, but she pulled away.

"How could you ruin my family like this?" she demanded. "My father loved you as the son you were to be to him! And now, you lead the charge in the destruction of his business."

"No, the Gods did that with that storm, not I."

"Shut up, you idiot!" the aged Catus yelled at his former self. "Cold-hearted bastard!"

"It is only business," Vesta said.

"My father is a kind and generous man, Catus Pompilius. A man who took you under his wing and taught you all you know. He honours the Gods, and they shall not forsake him or our family, even if you have." Junia's head straightened up, and her eyes became as cold as forged steel as she looked upon the wealthy wretch before her.

"Your father is now poor, and so are you…but I am willing to overlook it if you will marry me and never ask me to help him again."

The aged Catus hung his head at the words, the poison that issued from his own lips, and the retort that the young woman gave.

"I loved you with all my heart and soul, but now…I feel nothing but sadness and pity for the man I once knew, for he is gone forever from my heart, from my life." Junia looked the young Catus in the eyes one last time, her own eyes pools of watery sadness and grief that would wrench the heart of the hardest man, unless he were Catus himself. "The young man of honour I once knew, and who loved me, is lost. Were he here, I would marry him, but he is not, and my soul will grieve for him. My place is with my family, Catus Pompilius, and not with a man who prizes a denarius above all else. May the Gods forgive you…"

Before the young Catus could speak a word more, Junia had turned and walked away, disappearing into the crowd.

"Come back, Junia!" old Catus cried, his eyes running with tears. "I was wrong!" he shouted. "I was wrong…"

The steps of the temple of Venus and Rome swam beneath his feet then and they were suddenly at the gates of a villa on the prosperous Quirinal Hill.

"What place is this now?" he asked the goddess, snifling and wiping his eyes as he peered through the bars of that property, gazing upon the manicured gardens where fountains sparkled and danced and peacocks roamed among ivy-covered columns of pure pink and white marble.

Vesta did not answer, but allowed him to gaze for some time until the sound of laughter joined the scene before the sprawling villa.

There, in the garden, was Junia, as graceful and beautiful a matron as Rome had ever seen.

"Junia!" Catus exclaimed. "But how… How lovely

and happy she looks!"

Junia laughed as she walked, and dancing behind her was a joyous brood of children, five in all, each of them adoring and attentive, each lighting up her eyes with love beyond measure. They were loud and raucous, and it appeared that Junia would have had it no other way.

"So many children!" Catus said. "What a noise they make!" He continued to watch as Junia and her brood skipped through the garden to a covered loggia where two older people sat smiling and holding hands.

"It's Peli," Catus said, observing the old man's smile, and the clean, crisp toga he wore beside his graceful wife, Melia, as they greeted their grandchildren. "But how…"

It was as if the sun rose and set daily in that garden, so great was the happiness there, the joy, the love of that family.

"I don't understand," Catus began to say just as the gates of the villa were thrown open by the slaves and a horse came trotting onto the path leading to the villa.

"Father!" the children yelled as they rushed the horseman.

"Konstantin Modestus," Catus observed, feeling

bitter jealousy begin to seep into his veins. "He always did envy my time with Junia," he said.

"He loved her very deeply for years," Vesta said. "And he cared for her family, seeking to repay the kindness Peli had always shown him."

"Io Saturnalia!" Modestus cried to his rushing children, all of them falling into his arms and knocking him to the green grass in a jumble of laughter.

"Father!" they all cried. "Io! Io! Io!"

"No more work for seven days, my loves!" he said as he kissed each of them and rose to embrace Junia.

"Thank the Gods you're home safely," she said before she pressed her lips to his.

"It was a successful trip, and one that will secure the fortunes of our family for some time. The new ships are stronger and more seaworthy than the old ones, the captains more reliable." Konstantin turned to Peli and Melia as they approached. "Io Saturnalia, mother...father." They all greeted each other warmly.

"May the Gods bless these days," Junia said as they all turned to go into the villa and begin the celebrations in earnest.

Catus stepped forward, unspeaking, trying to catch

Junia's eyes, to glimpse the happiness and light in them that he had forgotten, but even as he reached her, she turned, and arm-in-arm with her husband, she and her family were walking away down the path to the villa where song and light now poured out of every window and doorway.

The bitter old man turned on the goddess, his anger seething, masking the pain that erupted in his heart, in his gut, in every inch of his person from head to foot and the root of his very soul.

"How can you do this to me? Why show me all of this?" he demanded, facing the goddess and casting his eyes at the fiery bowl that yet burned brightly before her.

"For pity's sake, Catus Pompilius…"

"Pity? I've no need for your pity, or that accursed blinding light!" Catus tried to kick at the flaming bowl, but his feet stopped short of every blow. "Leave me alone!" he wailed. "I've no need of you or the pain you shine your bleeding light on! Leave me alone!"

Vesta nodded and turned her back on Catus Pompilius then, and the world went black and cold, and he found himself alone in the lararium of his domus once more.

He shivered as his watery eyes opened in the darkness of that mournful storage shrine. Catus pushed himself to his feet and stepped out of the room into the moonlit garden of the peristylium. He suddenly longed for fire, and felt that his home was never darker or colder than it was in that very moment.

"Junia…" he muttered as he stumbled around the colonnade to the stairs and up. "I'm so tired," he said as he fell onto the couch in his cubiculum to succumb to the dark. "Curse you, Krelis… Curse you…"

IV

THE SECOND IMMORTAL

Catus awoke with such a start that he nearly propelled himself into the air, off of the couch, and onto the floor. He sweat profusely and felt the cold deep in his bones, a lonesome cold, the sort from which one felt there was no escape, nor ever would there be.

He squinted, unable to see anything. The darkness of his room was so complete and deep that he feared for a moment that he had gone blind with all of the strain of his nightmares. When a cloud passed away from its place before the moon outside his window, he felt a relief such as never before. That is until he remembered the words of his imagined Krelis.

There was supposed to be a second immortal.

"Wrong as ever, Krelis," he muttered, settling back down beneath the thin blanket.

He closed his eyes and was nearly asleep once more when the house began to shake with laughter.

It was a great, explosive, joyous laughter the likes of which Catus had never heard before. The strain of the sound seemed to wend its way about his cubiculum and surround him, attempting to pierce its way into his mind, and he felt it difficult to resist, so pure and lustful it was.

Then Catus noticed the light in the courtyard below, a brilliance that lit the walls up to the rooftop of the second story within the peristylium.

"What in Hades is going on?" he growled, rising and making his way to the railing overlooking the dried-up garden. The laughter burst forth once more and Catus leaned over the railing to see light pouring from the triclinium below. "Who's there? Ida?"

"Catus Pompilius!" a great, booming voice called. "Come down here!"

Catus said nothing, but moved quietly down the stairs, his anger fizzling into curiosity, for the brightness radiating from the triclinium intensified the closer he got. When he reached the bottom of the stairs, the laughter was accompanied by the soft playing of reed pipes and the rattle of sistra. He stepped into the doorway, but had to clamp his eyes shut for all the brightness.

"Enter my world, mortal man, and see the joy that there is to be had!" The voice was everywhere in the domus, before and beside Catus, and behind him, pushing him into the room.

Catus sniffed and found the air to be delectable and mouth-watering. "What is this? Who are you?" Slowly, he opened his eyes, and the astonishment nearly knocked him from his feet.

"Ha, ha, ha!" the voice laughed. "Come before me, Catus Pompilius!"

The dark and unused triclinium that Catus usually ignored in his day-to-day business was utterly transformed. Candles and lamps burned everywhere, lighting up a gleaming green and white marble floor, and the walls, oh the walls! They were no longer black and crumbling, but the faint echoes of colour and scene that had graced them in previous years had now come to life. It was with amazement that Catus observed the vast forest scene where trees swayed and their leaves winked, where flowers grew in bursts of colour and the water of fountains ran clear and cool into moonlit pools. Shock grabbed hold of him once more as other movements in the wood caught his eyes.

Upon and within those painted walls, satyrs and

maenads danced among the trees, their music reaching Catus' ears as they twirled and laughed and frolicked and waved for him to join them. He blinked several times and rubbed his eyes.

"I am over-tired," he told himself, only to be answered by the great laughter again.

"Now, look upon me!"

Slowly, Catus turned and there before him was Bacchus himself, larger than life, upon a couch of gold decked with multi-hued cushions. His ivy and holly-encircled head nearly touched the ceiling of the triclinium, and his eyes looked down upon Catus like two brilliant blue stars set in the night sky. Great, soft curls of auburn hung about his powerful shoulders, and his beard lay upon his chest, which was just visible in the middle of his colourful tunic of red and green.

Catus was indeed hard-put to gaze upon the immortal for too long and began to cower and edge away, clearly unused to such a scene as that.

"Do not fear, Catus Pompilius," Bacchus said. "This is a time of celebration and joy for all. Come, drink!" He then held out a cup of purest gold that matched his own that was filled with rich, dark, unwatered wine.

"I cannot," Catus muttered as he held the brilliant

cup. "Wine does not agree with me."

"Drink!" Bacchus commanded, smiling wide beneath his beard.

Catus gazed at the walls all about him to see the satyrs and maenads all holding up their own cups in his direction and shouting 'Io!' to him. With trembling hands he drank, and no nectar in all of his days could have been sweeter than that. He gulped it thirstily, as if he had been lost in the sand seas of Africa Province without water for a week.

"That's better!" Bacchus said.

Catus felt clarity come over him, his spirits lifted, and his body younger and absent pain. He looked on Bacchus again and noted the mountains of food laid out as if it were a banquet awaiting the Olympian gods themselves. There were platters of steaming breads and fresh cheeses, figs, dates, grapes and oranges piled high and begging to be eaten, and among them, honeyed pastries dripping with sweetness.

Then there were spits turning of their own accord over bright fires - wild boar, roast goat and sheep, and delicate game birds succulent in smell and taste.

Catus licked his lips at the scene and was about to ask for more wine when he noticed that his cup was already full again.

"I think you have been starving yourself for an age, Catus Pompilius!" Bacchus exclaimed, his voice pitying. "You do not really know me, do you?"

"You are Bacchus, God of Wine and frivolity?"

"Frivolity?" Bacchus sat up, his muscular legs swinging down over the edge of the couch. "Would you call making the most of the life the Gods give you frivolous? Beware, mortal man, for you do not even know what living is."

"Forgive me, oh Bacchus," Catus stuttered beneath the god's pointed finger.

"Do not fear me, Catus Pompilius, for I am here to show you what living is. Living is eating and drinking…" he gestured to the banquet and wine cup clasped in Catus' hand. "It is music, dancing and singing!" He then pointed to the lively paintings where the satyrs and maenads twirled ecstatically. "And it is so much more than you could possibly understand."

Bacchus looked up to the ceiling and there the stars swirled about the moon, and the constellations came to life - Centaurus and Cygnus, Pegasus and the Didyma - all of them moving about the night sky as alive as Catus was in that moment. Bacchus then looked back to Catus and placed his hand upon the man's shoulder.

"I do not understand…why me?" Catus asked, the wine cup falling away from his mouth.

"Oh, Catus Pompilius," Bacchus said, as a wise adult to a child. "Do not question the ways of this universe, for there is more life in the mysteries of this world and the next than in the cold reason by which you live. Come…" he said, gesturing to the frescoed walls where an ancient ship bobbed in the water of a river running through the wood, "…I will show you."

Bacchus then held out his hand to Catus, who took it reluctantly, and pulled him into the painting and onto the ship.

Catus gasped as his triclinium became a painting set in the deep wood of the forest, and the satyrs and maenads approached like skittish deer in a glade to sniff at the mortal man.

They all bowed before Bacchus, those spirited Bacchantes, and waved as their god and the mortal in tow settled themselves in the ship amid cushions, vines of black and yellow grapes draped from the mast and along the sides.

"Let me show you the world you are missing!" Bacchus said before the ship floated away without the aid of wind or oar.

Catus fell down, laughing as they sped away, trying to steady himself and drink more from the cup that was full again.

They were now sailing through the night, high above the Tiber, looking down upon Rome where a million lights burned brightly as if in a terrestrial firmament. They circled the city as if upon the wings of a great eagle swooping and rising, even as they drank wine from their golden cups.

Often, Catus found the god roaring with laughter, or nodding in admiration at something, but he could never quite tell the reason for his jollity. "What day is it that so many are awake and revelling, though it be the middle of the night?"

"Why, it is the eve of the start of Saturnalia in Rome! Io Saturnalia!" Bacchus roared.

"Saturnalia?" Catus grew sullen, and the god stared at him.

"Yes. Now drink, and do not be yourself for once," Bacchus laughed again.

Catus drank and smiled awkwardly, as if unused to straining the muscles of his face outwardly. "Is it the past?" he asked.

"No. This is the present...Saturnalia as it is at this moment in time."

"Will they not see us or hear you roaring from these heights?"

"We shall be unseen, as you were when the good goddess Vesta led you about." Bacchus clapped his hands and pointed to the East. "Look you!"

Catus leaned upon the mast of the ship, drinking from his wine cup and tasting the juice-filled grapes that hung beside his face there. He was about to ask what he was looking for when a sliver of pure light appeared on the horizon and the world was painted with colour that swept from the Palace of the Sun as the great charioteer sped through the heavens on his daily circuit.

"Io Saturnalia!" Bacchus yelled, and as if in deliberate co-ordination, voices far below shouted the same.

Catus stared over the rail of the ship to see the Forum Romanum and a great crowd gathering far below. "What is it?" he asked. "What is happening?"

"It is the official start of the festival," Bacchus said solemnly. "It begins with the sacrifice at the Temple of Saturn. Look you, for I suspect that you have never seen such a thing."

"I cannot see so far distant," Catus complained.

"Then I will show you!" Bacchus said, pulling on the rudder of the ship and sending them into a dive which landed them beside the newly unveiled Arch of Septimius Severus. Once the ship had set itself down and Bacchus and Catus were upon land, it disappeared from their sight.

God and mortal man moved through crowd as wraiths until they were at the very front of the throng, and then walking up the vast stairs to the temple. There, before the great doors of the temple, stood an altar of purest black, around which were gathered several priests, all of them with their heads uncovered.

"Why do they not wear a fold of their togas over their heads, as is usual?" Catus asked.

"It is the ritus graecus," Bacchus answered, his voice deep and low as he peered beyond the priests to the inside of the temple. "This is a day of opposites, Catus Pompilius, therefore they perform the rites uncovered.

"And what do they sacrifice?"

"Do you know nothing of this day?" Bacchus shook his head and his long hair danced about his thick shoulders. "A suckling pig is the offering of choice for Saturn. But there is more... Look!" Bacchus pointed into the temple interior, and suddenly they were standing beyond the priests in the fire-lit space before the main altar and statue of Saturn.

Outside, the crowd had grown silent and respectful, their heads bowed as they gazed upon the priests who placed a young piglet upon the altar, pouring grains of wheat upon its head before the knife slashed deeply into its neck. There was no squeal, no sound, as the priests went about their work.

Then, inside, three more priests of Saturn began to unbind great swathes of wool from about the feet of the cult statue. Once the feet were bared, a smaller statue was placed upon a small litter and they carried it upon their shoulders to the pronaos of the temple and out into the sunshine, their feet wading through the small pool of blood about the outer altar.

Catus and Bacchus stood at the doorway, looking out at the faces of Rome, silent in the one moment, and then exploding into a cheer that splashed like a great wave throughout the Forum Romanum.

"Io Saturnalia!" they all shouted, including the priests. "Io Saturnalia! Io Saturnalia!"

Then, the entire populace that was packed into the

heart of Rome writhed and wriggled and laughed their way to the long tables that had been set out the length of the forum for the convivium publicum. At the same time, the image of Saturn himself was paraded into their midst to rest upon the stairs of the Senate opposite the temple, to preside over the public feast.

"What a waste of public funds!" Catus muttered, and Bacchus turned upon him.

"A waste? Why, it is the public who benefits from this very feast. And it pleases Saturn to see them dine and live gloriously as they did in his day."

Catus turned back to look at the temple and there he thought he spied a black-robed figure with a long staff going back into the temple. He would have questioned Bacchus about it, but he thought better of it, fearing the utterance of the words that came to his mind in that moment.

"The people of Rome are pleased," Bacchus said.

"Of course they are, when the dies festus declares three days of no work while still earning wages! It's ridiculous!"

"Walk!" Bacchus commanded. "And drink!" He plunged ahead along the tables of Romans, young and old, foreign and not, as they ate and drank, slave and citizen side by side. They saw entire families eating together, their children's faces lit by smiles that rarely made an appearance for all the hunger they experienced. Groups of friends huddled and joked and rolled dice, couples with eyes only for each other luxuriated in a day together without work, and those with not a soul to speak with the days of their lives talked and laughed with the strangers beside them at those vast communal tables.

"They do seem happy, don't they?" Catus said, a sliver of jealousy inching its way into his dried-up old heart.

"There is more," Bacchus said, touching Catus' arm.

Suddenly, they were in the middle of the markets of Trajan, amid stalls piled high with all manner of foods to be purchased that day by Romans of every station, to be eaten over the seven days of Saturnalia.

There were mountains of nuts - chestnuts, walnuts, almonds, hazelnuts and more - piled in mounds for all to see, to be eaten and also gambled with, as was tradition. There were fruits of the season - apples, pears, sanguine oranges from the region around Baiae to the South, and the last of the season's plump and juicy figs. Amphorae of olives and wine from Etruria were popular with those going about their special marketing, as were joints of cured meat, sausages and more. By far, the most popular stalls were those specializing in suckling pigs for Saturnalia, more affordable to most than whole wild boar, peacocks and swans favoured by the richer citizens of Rome.

Garum, the fish sauce that would douse the meat upon any table in Rome, was at the top of every person's shopping list, be it from Iberia or Leptis Magna in Africa Proconsularis, and the row of sellers of this Roman favourite were busier now than any time of year.

Catus watched as Bacchus led him through the maze of the market, moving from food and drink stalls to the textile sellers where multi-coloured sythesia were hanging, tempting passers-by with a new set of clothing for the occasion to replace the regular tunic or toga. There were also leather and wool pilei, the conical hats that men wore during Saturnalia, and Catus noticed that most of the men around them were already wearing them, so many in fact that for a moment he felt as though he were in some faraway foreign market along the Silk Road.

They then came to stalls where sigillaria were being sold, those traditional gifts of Saturnalia that were of no great expense, but supremely popular among all classes and between masters and slaves. Wax cerei were sold in bundles, both thick and thin, of tallow or bees wax. There were writing tablets and dice, knucklebones, combs, and toothpicks. There were various types of hats and pipes, knives and axes, lamps, balls, and, a few particular stalls in one area were busy with sweaty husbands trying to buy perfumes for their wives and mistresses.

In another area, toys for children were being sold - dolls, toy horses, balls, wooden swords, and much more to make any child cartwheel or shriek with a joyful 'Io!' through the atrium of their domus.

And everywhere Bacchus passed, the unseeing people burst into song or laughter, their lives lit up by his presence and passing, and the general gaiety of the season. The god enjoyed the effect he had on every person, pointing out the joy that suffused every single Roman on that first day of the festival.

As they passed the sellers of holly and ivy, both of which were carefully carried away in great bundles to their homes, or the homes of their masters, Bacchus stopped and stared at Catus.

"What do you think of all this, Catus Pompilius?" he gestured with a great sweep of his hand, his broad chest and arms open wide as if he were presenting a kingdom to a foreign visitor.

Catus nodded and rubbed his hands excitedly. "There certainly is a lot of buying and selling," he said, his ear catching the sound of clinking coins which he had been noticing the entirety of their market journey.

"Is that all you have an eye for?" Bacchus asked, shaking his head.

"No," he said, his voice defensive. "I also notice that idle people spend more. If they were busy, they would not tumble into debt so much if they were not home celebrating rather than working."

"Oh, you are a sad mortal!" The god then carried on walking, his wine cup brimming as he went, leaving joyful banter in his wake.

Catus tripped along after him, weaving in and out of the groups of people who took no notice of the wraith in their midst.

"Where are we going?" Catus asked.

"Why, to a neighbourhood you know well, Catus Pompilius!" Bacchus turned down a street that was much narrower than the previous thoroughfares. The sun disappeared behind towering tenement blocks that appeared to lean over the road, and the light that graced the cobbles of the street now came from the candles people had lit and set outside of their doors, coupled with what meagre decorations they could afford.

"Why are we in the Suburra?" Catus asked. "I've no wish to be here."

"Why not? You own half of it, do you not?" Bacchus asked, ploughing ahead. "These are your people!" Bacchus pointed to a family begging at one of the crossroads, then to a lame veteran who turned over garbage in the gutter, hoping to find some half-rotted piece of food to sustain his cramped gut. As Bacchus passed these sad citizens of Rome's poorest district, others stopped in their passing to hand the family an entire loaf of bread and a blanket, or to offer a hearty hand shake and a stick of cooked meat to the scrounging warrior who had served Rome's legions far to the East and been maimed for it.

Catus was silent as he spied this, his eyes searching ahead, beyond the scene immediately before him, but Bacchus lingered, leaned over to see into the eyes of the family and of the veteran, and the smiles, however brief, that passed over their visages for the kindness showed to them by those who were not much more fortunate than themselves.

They walked on and finally came to a stop in the courtyard of a particular grouping of tenements. The courtyard was hung with thin ivy and holly garlands, and candles burned around the perimeter. In the centre, a few tables had been set out with a roasting pig upon a spit in the centre. About the tables, young children raced and played at tag while a few women sat laughing and talking together while their husbands sat at drink and a friendly game of dice. All caught up on news for they did not usually see each other, though they were neighbours, for they worked hard every day and were rarely together.

"This is your largest property, is it not?" Bacchus said to Catus.

"Yes," Catus replied, stepping forward and looking around. "Several of these people were late with their rents." He turned to the fire over which the pig cooked and crackled. "How could they afford such a feast as this?"

"This 'feast', as you call it," Bacchus said, sitting upon one of the long benches, "will feed everyone here but a little. They come together for each other's company, and to honour the Gods."

"But the fire is hazardous and liable to burn down the entire tenement. My property!"

"Hush," Bacchus soothed. "You need not worry, for the fire is well tended and the meat shall not burn." He pointed, and there on the other side of the fire was a young boy, skinny and lame with one leg at an odd angle, tending the fire with care. He licked his lips as he turned the spit a half-turn, but he did not sneak a bite. He took his charge seriously, and called out any of the other rushing children before they were able to steal a sliver of meat. He laughed, but then it turned into a cough that eventually subsided. The short struggle evidently took a toll upon his little body. He combed back his raven-black hair, and sighed, getting back to his work.

"They set a lame child to tend the entire feast?" Catus asked in amazement.

"He is as stout and trustworthy as his father, I daresay," Bacchus said, nodding toward the broad wooden staircase that led up to the fifth floor of that wooden shambles.

Coming down, a man carried an old woman in his arms, unable as she was to make it down the flights of stairs for the feast.

"Io Saturnalia!" the women and men in the courtyard called to the old mother as she was carried by her hero.

"Why's it's my collector, Giles Amadea!" Catus said. "What is he doing?"

"He is helping his fellow citizen!" Bacchus retorted. "Is that not obvious? In fact, he helps all of them as much as he can, in any way that he can."

"After he collects their rents, I should hope."

Bacchus ignored Catus as he watched Giles set the old mother down in the only chair with a back. Two of the women came over to cover her legs with a blanket and sit to speak with her, the other women following suit and she, the old woman, now at the centre of their converse, a broad smile upon her lips and a cup of watered acetum set in her trembling hands.

Catus watched Giles go over to throw a pair of dice once with the other men and they all laughed at his misfortune. Paying up his share of hazelnuts, he patted them on the shoulders and went to the centre of the courtyard to see his son.

"Paulus, my boy!" Giles said as he sat down beside his youngest child. "I think that nowhere in Rome is there a finer cook than you. I could smell your fine work all the way up at the top of the stairs before the curtain of mother Cassia's doorway!"

"Thank you, Father!" The boy beamed as he looked upon Giles, and his father ruffled his hair and kissed the top of his head. "I'm sure there are much better cooks than I in Rome!" he laughed. It was a sound as playful as a summer fountain, and as melancholy as a soft reed pipe at sunset.

Catus took notice of the intimate scene between them, and thought of his own father, how such a scene as that had never once, in all his youth, ever played out. "He loves his son, doesn't he?" Catus said.

"He would die for him, verily," Bacchus said. "In fact, Giles Amadea would die for any member of his family. They hold this community together, look you!"

Bacchus nodded in the direction of the ground-floor apartment, the largest in the tenement, but by far not the richest of the Suburra, if 'rich' were a word one could use in that wasteland of Rome. From out of the door, came Marcia Amadea, Giles' wife, and her three daughters, the twins Calida and Callula, and their eldest, Diana. Each of them carried humble wooden platters covered in small mushroom pies, nearly-limp greens, bread, cheese and olives, and a steaming platter with three roast chickens upon it. They paraded into the courtyard with great ceremony and applause as if they were with the emperor in his triumph parading the spoils of war. Except, these were the combined spoils of the entire tenement's hard labour. Behind them came the second eldest Amadea, Lucian, his lean, strong arms carrying a basket of blushing apples. He called to the other boys like a parade ground centurion to come and help him distribute his wealth along the tables to ensure that every one enjoyed their share.

"Apples go especially well with suckling pig," his mother heard him say to his fellows, a secret she had told him before they exited their home.

Catus watched Marcia Amadea move among the throng, her smile radiant and welcoming to all, even though her stola was faded and worn, the same as her husband's synthesis. She was obviously a friend among friends in that place, and Catus could not help but smile as he looked upon her with her children.

"Giles has quite a brood. It's no wonder he cannot put away much coin."

"Drink, Catus Pompilius," Bacchus said. "Giles Amadea is a man of honour in this place, and what's more, he does not know it. He does what he can for his family and his fellow citizens. What matter the savings of coin when a man is such as he?"

"I only mean that with such a large family, he might be hard-pressed is all." Catus' voice was not harsh now, but rather unnaturally soft, less critical than concerned.

"He does what he can with his meagre wages," Bacchus said, not looking at Catus, but laughing as Giles lifted young Paulus upon his shoulders to a cheer from the assembly.

"To the best cooks in Rome!" Giles yelled. "Marcia and Paulus Amadea!"

"Io Saturnalia!" the neighbours all cried together.

They all grew quiet then as cups were filled for each and everyone had theirs in hand.

A young Etrurian man, who lived there among them, a haruspex new to the college in Rome, stepped into the centre with a wooden frame and held it up to the sky.

"Oh Saturnus," he began. "God of earth and the sowing of seeds…we honour you this day." The young man poured wine over the suckling pig and it sizzled in the ashes and flame beneath, sending smoke up into the air. All about the courtyard, others poured a little of their wine or water upon the ground and gazed up.

The haruspex held up his wooden frame to watch the smoke circle and waft upward, even as a flock of pigeons swept by from right to left.

There was a collective gasp, and then a relaxed exhale as he smiled.

"Saturn favours our feast," the haruspex said. "Io Saturnalia!"

"Io Saturnalia!" everyone cheered, young Paulus loudest of all. He was no doubt happy that he could finally taste the meat he had been smelling and turning over for hours.

At that moment, everyone sat where they could and the humble feast began. Candles were lit, music was played, and laughter echoed to the rickety rooftops of Catus' largest tenement.

"What do you think, Catus Pompilius?" Bacchus said.

Catus was silent a moment, his eyes having rested upon Giles and his family as they laughed and ate together, as they spoke with all around them. Then he spoke. "They are a close group, the lot of them."

"They are. They have to be."

"They have made quite merry with but a little food divided amongst many." He nodded approvingly. "Quite sensible."

"They are," Bacchus said, "as they must be. "They are, none of them, perfect beings, but they toil as best they can with what the Gods have given them, for such is the fate of each and every one of them. They know joy and sorrow, love and hate, but they live as best they can. If there is one perfect being among them, it is young Paulus."

"Paulus? How is he perfect?" Catus asked, clearly confused by the god's statement. "His poor body is broken...he is sick and small. How will he survive in such a state? He is not perfect." Catus felt great sadness then, unfamiliar as it was.

"His young heart is pure," Bacchus said. "The boy never complains or utters a false or hateful word. His optimism inspires his family, which he loves above all, and he honours the Gods in his heart. Were all mortals as *lame* as he, Rome's empire would be a splendid and peaceful place from end to end."

Catus noted with a tightening in his heart, that Giles and Marcia flanked their little son warmly the entire time, and that he never wanted for a kind and loving touch or word from either of them or his siblings. They were a family such as he had never had or dared to dream of.

"I wish..." Catus was about to say.

"What do you wish?" Bacchus said.

"I wish...I... My nephew...he came to my home yesterday. I...spoke very ill to him, though he had done me no harm."

"Is that regret I hear in your voice, Catus

Pompilius?"

Catus nodded reluctantly. "I suppose it is."

"Regret is time wasted. Action is what matters among gods and men." Bacchus drank. "Look to your employee now, and learn…"

Catus watched as Giles kissed his wife and stood with a cup of wine in the middle of the gathering. Catus thought the ex-gladiator looked a little foolish wearing the colourful, patched synthesis and pointed pileus, but it did not affect the deference and respect the rest of the people there showed him when he stood in their midst.

"Friends! Neighbours…" Giles called out, laughing and smiling. "Io Saturnalia!"

"Io Saturnalia!" the gathering called back with a great cheer that rose to the rooftops and made Bacchus himself laugh.

"The Gods have indeed blessed us this day," he began more solemnly, "and I for one am full of gratitude for living among such excellent folk, and enjoying such excellent food." He raised his cup and drank with everyone. "I thank the Gods for my family." Here, a tender look at his wife and children as if, for a moment, they were the only ones present for him as he drank, then looked around the gathering. "I also know how tough times are here in Rome, and especially here in the Suburra."

At this, a quiet fell over the place as people agreed, nodding or hanging their heads. They all knew, though most tried to forget, that for only the three days of the dies festus, their lives took on a lustre that could not be darkened by poverty or cruelty, or the daily battle they each faced to scrounge a living for their families.

"Times are tough indeed," Giles continued, falling silent, his mind flashing painfully to one of the myriad fights upon the sands.

Catus flinched and fell backward, his head snapping from side to side as the very same images of blood, death and dying flashed in his mind.

Bacchus stared earnestly at him for a moment, and then back to Giles, whose eyes had shut tightly for a moment.

But he was calmed by the tiny hand that now gripped his.

Young Paulus stood feebly beside his father, leaning upon one of the nearby tables, looking up at him with bright, admiring eyes.

"I love you, my boy," Giles whispered to his son. "Thank you."

"I am grateful," Giles continued once more, "and I would raise my wine -"

"The finest vintage!" someone yelled, causing them all to laugh.

"Yes!" Giles answered. "And I would drink it in this moment to the man who gave me a living beyond the walls of the Colosseum, and who provides us with this palace in which we live. I drink to Catus Pompilius!"

There was silence... Complete and utterly confused silence.

Giles looked around, his cup stopping just short of his mouth.

In a moment, Marcia was up and standing beside Giles, leaning in to whisper quickly into his ear, the stray strands of her long hair about her face hanging before her now angry eyes.

"Are you trying to start a riot?" she told her husband. "How can you toast such a man as Catus Pompilius?"

Someone nearby heard her and spoke up. "She's right, Giles! How can we toast the man who extorts us monthly for the rents we pay for this shambles?" They looked up at the leaning wood and wattle tenements of their homes towering over them, as ready as a stack of summer kindling to go up in flames at any moment if they didn't fall on their heads first.

"He's a monster!" someone else yelled.

"While he lives it up on the Esquiline, we suffer disease and violence down here!"

There were various other shouts of the horrors and threats that Catus Pompilius had visited upon the hardworking people of the tenement, and it threatened to turn into a chorus of hate, that festive gathering.

"You certainly have got their attention over the years," Bacchus joked with Catus, though he did not laugh.

"I'm sorry, husband," Marcia said to Giles as he stood there gripping his son's hand.

"Quiet!" Giles suddenly roared, and the shouting died down. "You're all right, of course. Catus Pompilius can be mean and horrible, but he is quite alone and always has been. And look at us! We have friends…our families, and so much more. The Gods have blessed us!"

There were a few nods at this, for ingratitude was not something that those people fell in for. They were Romans, some from old Plebeian families.

"At Saturnalia," Giles said, "things are different. They are the opposite of what they usually are. And so, I say today, at this moment, we are the senators and finest Palatine ladies that Rome has ever seen!"

There was a cheer at this, and the rest of Giles' brood gathered around him.

"And on this day, the Gods would be pleased if we drink to the man who causes us so much misery."

There were no shouts this time.

"To Catus Pompilius!" Giles shouted, and this time, the toast was taken up with furious passion by the rest.

"To Catus Pompilius!"

"May the Gods bless him!" young Paulus said to his mother and father and they hoisted him between them and kissed his pale cheeks.

As music upon a pipe and on the voice of many a man and woman there struck up, Catus stepped forward, between his dancing tenants, to look at the boy Paulus. He had heard his last words a moment before, and his heart was wrenched in his chest.

Bacchus was at his shoulder. "I hope you heard that child just now, Catus Pompilius."

"I…I did…yes." Catus looked at Giles and his family. "Is the boy…is he very ill?"

"Yes," Bacchus said flatly. "The services of a medicus are expensive in Rome, and Giles Amadea cannot pay all he needs to. Your nephew has offered aid to them, but he is not Midas, or a god."

"Will young Paulus live?" Catus asked, turning from the boy to the god beside him. "Will he?"

"I see a dark shadow of mourning hanging over the people who live here, and a spear shaft through the heart of this family." He nodded toward Giles and his wife and children. The god smiled darkly then and Catus felt a chill. "Then again, what is one less rat in the Suburra? If more of them died, then so much the better for you!" Bacchus said, throwing Catus' own words into his face. "The Suburra would be a less pestilent place, and you could sell this tenement for a fortune!"

Catus stood before Bacchus as shamed as he had ever felt. He was angry with the god, but he remained silent, his eyes instead drawn once more to Giles and his son Paulus, and the merry scene, before it all faded into mist and they found themselves standing in a fire-lit street of the Caelian Hill.

The Caelian Hill was much louder than the Esquiline, the houses fine and tasteful, but more pressed together. The atmosphere, however, was absolutely jovial. Crowds of revellers walked about with torches or lit candles, and many a Roman man and woman bellowed a hearty 'Io Saturnalia!' from afoot or from the comfort of bedecked and perfumed litters.

Songs were being sung from the heart, and drink flowed freely past everyone's lips as they passed from one well-meaning domus to the next.

Catus walked beside Bacchus, his mind still upon the scene they had just departed, when a great peal of laughter, the most joyful Catus had ever heard, escaped the confines of one particular domus, spreading into the street to urge others on in merriment, just for their being in proximity to such a celebration.

"What goes on at such parties?" Catus asked the god of wine and revelry.

"Why they eat and drink, sing and joke, laugh and make love. There is no ill will present during Saturnalia in most of these homes," Bacchus said, stopping before the street-front door of the great laughing house. "Come, Catus Pompilius! Let's go in!" Bacchus said, making for the doorway.

"Oh no, I couldn't, oh Bacchus. It would not be

proper to go uninvited into a stranger's domus."

Bacchus smiled. "Oh, you are not uninvited." Then he went in, pulling Catus' old grey toga sleeve as he went through the wall.

They found themselves in a small atrium, freshly painted in red and white with a thick green stripe midway up the wall. In the small impluvium, burning candles floated, casting a reflective light upon the ceiling.

Several guests stood about with red Samian cups in hand, drinking and talking, laughing and generally enjoying each other's company.

Then the great laughter that could be heard outside burst from the triclinium beyond the garden and the entire assembly roared with joy.

Catus laughed along too, unable to help himself, and Bacchus joined him, rubbing the old man's bald head as they weaved a ghostly path through the thickening crowd of drinkers.

"I do believe I know that laugh," Catus said, peering over and around people to catch a glimpse of the laugh's originator.

Bacchus stopped just inside the doorway to the triclinium and leaned against the wall. In the middle of that room of decent dimension, its walls painted like a forest in Elysium, there sat Julian Corbin, Catus' own nephew, beside a woman that could only have been his wife, Viola, a smiling, dark beauty.

"Julian!" Catus cried, waving, forgetful of his own invisibility.

"Listen!" Bacchus said, casting his arm over the group and giving birth to a great round of joy and mirth.

Julian was wearing the brightest, most elaborate and fickle synthesis anyone had ever seen, and the pointed pileus upon his head could have speared a gamecock were he to lean too closely to peer at it. His cheeks were absolutely rosy with wine and aglow with the good faith and wishes of every one of his guests.

Lamps burned everywhere, and smiling slaves wearing garlands about their heads passed to and fro with platters of food and pitchers of wine to ensure that every guest did not see themselves faced with an empty plate or cup. Some of the slaves were bid to sit down and drink while one of the guests, or indeed Julian himself, took a round of serving the great u-shaped formation of the couches.

"He takes the place of his slaves?" Catus was appalled.

"It's Saturnalia, Catus!" Bacchus reminded him. "It is traditional. Your nephew and his wife served a banquet quite as rich as this to all of their servants earlier this evening, and soon, on the day of the sigillaria, they will give them gifts too!"

"Preposterous!" Catus bellowed, the word turning bitter in his mouth before he spoke it.

"Is it?" Bacchus enquired, his great bearded face looking down on the mortal man. "Is it so rude an act to raise up those whose lives are in our care, who are a part of one's familia, for at least a few days out of the entirety of the year?"

"I suppose it is not," Catus relented. In that moment, the pale, skinny form of Ida came to his mind, and he felt a hint of shame.

Bacchus continued speaking, not looking at Catus, but rather as if he were thinking aloud. "Rather, the man who could act in such a way to those around him the whole year, through the length of his days on this earth, now he...he...would have indeed found the secret to joy in life."

Catus looked up at Bacchus and saw the great spark of life in his smile and godly eyes, eyes which, he noted, looked approvingly upon his own nephew, Julian.

"No, he isn't so bad as all that," Julian was saying, the conversation only then coming into Catus' hearing. "Why, I know, he holds half of Rome in thrall, and he can be the most dismal human being you have ever met!"

"That's understating it, Julian!" someone yelled from the far end of the room.

"Yes, quite!" Julian laughed. "'The Dead to dine on Saturnalia!' he actually said to me yesterday. And he meant it most wholeheartedly!"

"Well, I for one am glad that your uncle Catus is mistaken," Viola said beside her jubilant but suddenly thoughtful husband. "For as I look around this room, I see that we are all very much alive!"

Everyone cheered the hostess and domina of the house, and her husband kissed her lovingly upon the cheek where she reclined beside him.

"We are indeed alive, my love!" Julian said. "And, despite what every person I meet tells me, I do believe that my dear Uncle Catus Pompilius is too!"

There were disbelieving shouts at that from around the room, but Julian shushed them down with his happy smile.

"Is that why you reserve the lectus medius for

him?" asked one of Julian's close friends who sat nearby, nuzzling the woman beside him.

"Yes. It is," Julian answered.

Catus stepped forward between the standing guests behind the couches so that he could see into their midst the layout of the couches, and there he saw that the dining couch reserved for high-status guests, the lectus medius, indeed lay empty, piled high as it were with colourful and comfortable pillows, the best in the house, and the table before it set with the only silver plate ware Julian and his wife owned.

"He reserves the seat of honour for me?" Catus asked, turning to Bacchus. "Every year at Saturnalia?"

The god nodded and smiled.

Catus turned back to his nephew.

"But why do such a thing, Julian?" another of his friends asked. "Surely the lectus medius should go to…Senator Dio, for instance!" The man gestured to the older senator a few couches down, but the latter waved him off.

"I am quite comfortable where I am!" Senator Dio said.

"I'll tell you why I do such a thing," Julian

continued. "Because my mother…may the Gods grant her eternal joy…she loved her brother dearly, most fervently, in fact! By all accounts, my grandfather was as cruel as you could get, and my mother mourned the day that she and my uncle were torn apart."

The gathering grew quite quiet then, so much so that the very light of the fires seemed to dim in obeisance.

"Her last words in this world to me were to speak of love, and of my uncle Catus." Julian paused, his words failing him for the first time that night as he gripped his wine cup. But he rallied himself, oh yes. He was as strong as ever his mother was. "And so…that is why I reserve this couch for him. It is out of love…and hope…and the spirit of Saturnalia itself, that it remains empty until the day he pounds upon the door of my domus."

"Then we should drink to Catus Pompilius!" Viola raised her cup to the room. "For if enough of us wish him well this night, perhaps he might, just might, hear our collective voices."

"To Uncle Catus!" Julian bellowed.

"To Uncle Catus!" everyone echoed.

At that moment, more food and wine made the

rounds of the couches and the guests in the garden and atrium, the fires were stoked, and musicians and dancers weaved a spell about the domus.

"Dear, sweet Octavia," Catus said, wishing his sister were before him then so that he might wrap his arms about her and lift her up, tell her how well she had done in raising so fine a son as he who now made the rounds to greet every person within his home, citizen and slave alike.

Catus followed Julian to a far corner of the garden where he stopped to look up at the moon, silver and bright in the night sky.

"I loved your mother with all my heart, Julian," Catus said to the unhearing man. "I would have thrown myself to my death were it not for her." He began to tremble, his eyes burning as he looked upon the young man before him, so reminiscent of the sister he missed like a light in the dark. "I miss her so much…" he wept there, in the shadows beside the nephew to whom he had never uttered a kind word.

Julian's eyes stared up at that moon, and silver rivers of tears ran down his cheeks.

The sight tore at Catus' heart.

"My love," came the soft voice of Viola. "Oh, my

love…do not weep. Your mother's shade is with us, always."

"Forgive me," he said, wiping his eyes. "I know. But why…why does he not come to dine with us? He is all that remains of my mother, and she asked me to care for him. But how can I when he wants nothing to do with me?"

"As always, we will hope, my love. I did not know your mother, but I know through you that she was the most hopeful person in this world. One day…one day."

Julian kissed his wife upon the cheek and his smile slowly returned with a sniffle and another sip of wine.

"You're right!" he said. "Hope it is!"

And together, they went back into the garden to speak with their guests and re-immerse their domus in laughter, love, and yes, hope.

Catus made to follow them, more upon his mind to say to his nephew, but Bacchus held him fast.

"No, Catus Pompilius. It is time to go."

"But I don't want to. I want to stay with him." Catus pulled at the god's arm, but Bacchus was not to be swayed.

The garden and domus began to fade and once more they were out in the street. There sat the vine-clad ship, waiting for them, its sail filling with air as Bacchus climbed in and pulled Catus in alongside him.

Without another word, the ship sailed into the starry night sky. They sped along verily then, not setting down, but coming upon scene after scene of Saturnalian festivity.

They sped across the land, over villages ablaze with firelight and song, in front of distant frontier forts where Rome's troops enjoyed a respite from war, their thoughts with loved ones as they gamed and sang and drank with their brothers-in-arms.

From the rail of that ship, Catus thought he could see the celebrations of Saturnalia the length and breadth of the Empire, from the gatherings along the great wall in Britannia, to the streets of Leptis Magna where the imperial family held a magnificent banquet. Catus spied the celebrations in an Iberian fishing village, nestled as it was in a small cove that looked out to the faraway blackness of the ocean beyond the Pillars of Hercules. Then, the next moment, they looked down upon the coves of pirates in Cilicia, and the cities of Alexandria and Caesarea and more, to see gatherings where good will ruled, and people enjoyed food and drink and fine company.

Candles burned the entirety of the world, and on the day of the sigillaria, gifts both large and small were exchanged between friends and lovers, husbands and wives, parents and children. No matter how small or crude the token, it always brought a smile and some added warmth in that dark time of year before the rebirth of Sol Invictus, that unconquerable sun that would, by its very nature, melt the hearts of those who allowed but one shaft into their midst.

Catus accepted another cup of wine from Bacchus and leaned back against the mast of the ship. He had seen enough, truly, and his mind was whirling with all that he wanted now to do...to say...and yes, even to celebrate!

But Bacchus' smile was gone as the ship steered once more toward Rome, a beacon of Saturnalian fire from the night sky.

"Are we finished so soon?" Catus asked, a sudden dread in his heart that he dared not try to explain.

"Our time together is ended, Catus Pompilius," Bacchus raised his cup to Catus and drank, and the mortal man did likewise, his cup not refilling of its own magical volition, but remaining empty.

"But...there is so much more to see!" Catus gripped the mast of the ship as it dove down toward Rome with frightful speed, down toward an unusual darkness. He could not have been more frightened were he headed into the jaws of Scylla and Caribdis.

The ship came to a standstill upon a dark road with no light about to brighten the ground. Only Bacchus' eyes blazed coolly in the dark as he stared upon Catus.

The mortal disembarked from the ship and looked up at the god.

"What shall I do? I don't know where I am." Catus said, looking up at Bacchus.

"What you do, is up to you, Catus Pompilius. However, your life is not your own at the moment, and so I wish you well."

"Not my own? Wait! Please, oh Bacchus! Do not desert me!"

"You are not alone, mortal man... You are never alone..." Bacchus nodded into the darkness beyond the line of the road to a place among numerous ashen-coloured monuments of the necropolis.

Catus felt his skin prickle most frighteningly as he watched the ship leave him. He turned slowly in the lonely dark just as the moon's rays illuminated the ground ahead.

There, walking toward him, was the third immortal.

V

THE THIRD IMMORTAL

The god Saturn himself stood there in the cold moonlight, staring at Catus Pompilius. He wore a long, ragged red tunic, and his old, muscled arms were bare, the light casting them in a pallid grey. He began to walk toward Catus, his steps slow, unhurried. He carried a great staff which, as he came closer, Catus noticed was not a staff, but the arm of a great scythe, the sort used to cut wheat in Etruria. The implement curved over his shoulders like a partial harvest moon.

Saturn's thick beard, and the thin hair upon his head were as white as the fresh snow upon the cypress trees that surrounded them in that city of the dead. His eyes were ancient and wise, but also held something wild and unrelenting.

Catus quaked as he looked upon that stately god for whom those holy days had been declared, and he felt something dreadful and awe-inspiring welling inside.

"You…you…are the third immortal," Catus managed to say, only daring to look in quick glances and not for any length of time. "You are…Saturn?"

The god stood close now, still. His muscles were as hard as mountain stone, and as weathered, but the great scythe appeared to hold no weight for him where it rested upon his shoulder. His eyes observed Catus closely, too closely, and then he nodded ever so slowly in response.

Catus nodded hurriedly. "I fear you, dread god, more than any other, but I am prepared to go wherever you will this night, for I know that the divine visits this night have an ordained purpose." Catus looked up into those eternal, rheumy eyes, wanting to plead but knowing full well that the immortal would be deaf to him. "I have learned much this night, and the thoughts that have assailed my heart have warmed me once again with a fire I thought long dead. Oh Saturn…I beg you, Lord of Harvest and Time, show me how I may redeem myself in your eyes."

The god stared down at Catus, harsh and scolding, but he said nothing still, as an old man whom time has robbed of the want for wasted speech.

"I…I understand…" Catus said. "I will follow.

At that moment, Saturn turned and walked along the moonlit road toward the city and the darkness about them melted into grey daylight.

They were in the Forum Romanum, along the arcade of the Basilica Julia. Senators, equestrians, lawyers and philosophers moved to and fro in the shadow of the basilica and nearby temple of Saturn. People argued and laughed, hustled and pleaded for whatever ailed them in their plight.

But Catus' eyes were drawn to three men in togas upon the steps of the basilica, their wrists and fingers gaudy with gold and jewels, their fulsome paunches betraying their history of rich dining in a world of starvation. Catus looked to Saturn and the god nodded as if to indicate he should listen to their conversation.

"I heard the Gods took him in his sleep," said one of the men.

"So did I!" exclaimed another. "Apparently his slave found him in the middle of the atrium, his face bloated and purple from swallowing his tongue."

"That's not what I heard!" said the third man. "What I heard was that one of the tenants whose family he evicted broke into his home in the night and slit his throat, right there in his cubiculum."

145

"Well, however it happened, all I know is that the man is dead," the first said.

"Are we sure though?" said the second. "Because if it is true, we'll want to move in as quickly as possible before the state scoops up all his properties."

"You don't think he left it all to anyone, do you?"

The third man shook his head and laughed "Not a chance. You see..." he leaned in conspiratorially, "...as soon as I heard he'd been dispatched, I went straight to the temple of Vesta to ask if there was a will for him."

"Well?" asked the other two. "What did the priestess' say?"

"No will under that name was ever submitted."

"That means his properties will go to the State," said the first man.

And the second added, "which means we should get to the praetor's offices first to make an early bid on his properties!"

"Precisely!" the second man said. "If we can add them to our own holdings, we'll own most of Rome!"

They all laughed together and hurried off to find the praetor.

Catus turned to Saturn, his face confused. "I don't understand what all that has to do with me?

Saturn nodded toward two more men who were approaching from the direction of the Curia across the way.

"Well, it has to be said..."

"What?"

"Rome will be a better place for his death."

"I find it difficult to argue with that," said one of the men. "Will there be a funeral and rites performed? No matter how despicable a person, we should pay our respects to the dead. Especially that one! We don't want his lemur hanging around."

They both made the sign against ill-omen, and continued walking past Catus, through Catus!

"I don't believe there will be a procession, nor any sacrifices made. He left no instruction, and he had no family as far as I know."

"I pictured his monument along the Via Appia as a sort of titanic carved fist!" one of the men laughed, but stopped himself.

"Or the Suburra in flames!" chuckled the other,

covering his mouth quickly.

The two men disappeared and faded from view, and Saturn walked on, his dark form cutting its way through the crowds of Rome, unseen, unfelt, unheard, and everywhere they went, Catus caught snatches of lively conversation among the rich and powerful and the poor and destitute alike, and they all referred in some way to the passing of a man, or equally horrible men, Catus could not tell which.

At one end of the Forum of Trajan, an auction was underway in which several properties were being sold off one by one, some for vast amounts, others for a pittance. In another area of the markets, a few people approached with bundles which they unloaded upon the counters of foreign traders in an attempt to get whatever they could for the items they brought hastily to the fore - gold chains, chairs, sheets, lamps, wax tablets and styli, braziers, and more.

For a moment, Catus thought he recognized some of the items, but then remembered that he had locked his home for the night, bolted every door solidly. He also knew that Ida was a light sleeper and that she would have raised an alarm should anyone have dared enter.

At the edge of the Suburra, they came to a slave auction where a small crowd had gathered to gawk as several merchants and a few collegia leaders tried to out bid each other on the slaves that were paraded past.

It was one of the worst areas of the Suburra, an area where not even Catus roamed generally, and he was not often frightened by anything, so he liked to think. But in that place, he was happy of his invisibility to those around him. Still, he was curious why the god behind him had led him there. He did not know or recognize any of the faces about him.

Catus pressed forward to see one young girl being led off by the rough-looking collegium fellow, and then the crowd burst out with laughter and mock cat-calls. He looked at the small wooden dais where the auctioneer held a chain that linked to a collar about the neck of a middle-aged woman. Normally, Catus would not have paid her any heed, but his eyes were drawn to her, trying to catch a glimpse.

When she looked up he gasped, for it was Ida!

"What? That's my slave!" he yelled, the people about him deaf to his furious cries. "Ida! What are you doing there? What's happened? Did someone break into the house while I've been away? Answer me!"

Ida's face was bruised and her dirty tunica ripped to expose her body to the crowd. She tried covering herself but the slaver holding the chain slapped her.

Catus pushed his way through the crowd and rushed up onto the dais, his fist swinging so hard at the slaver's face that the blow would have killed him instantly had it not passed through as though the face were a puff of swirling smoke. "I'll see you dead!" he said to the slaver. "If you sell her, or harm her again, you'll regret it."

He knelt down then in front of his slave, and his heart felt pity for her, a pity that surprised him, that hurt him as he gazed into her dark eyes. She was there, but not, as if she had retreated to some faraway place of safety while she underwent her ordeal.

At that moment, Saturn stepped forward and took hold of Catus' hand, holding it above Ida's head.

In that moment, images of a home in Ephesus burst upon Catus' thoughts, of Ida smiling, of her laughing with a loving husband and children, uncles and aunts and aged parents. He barely recognized her, for all the happiness she had. Then the images turned dark, and there were sounds of weeping and screaming as it was all taken from her. There was a burning house, the limp bodies of children and the still bodies of her husband and family. And then grasping hands and chains and tears…so many tears.

Catus yanked away as soon as Saturn released his

grip on him, and he looked into Ida's pooling eyes as she remembered.

"A bargain!" the auctioneer yelled at the crowd. "A Saturnalia bargain for any man brave enough to take this one into his domus!" There was laughter all about Catus. "And I guarantee the previous owner did very little with her!" Another peal of laughter. "We all know what he was like!"

"What is he saying?" Catus said, turning quickly to Saturn. "Previous owner? Who is this man who has passed into oblivion that I hear people tell of across all of Rome? She is still *my* slave, not someone else's!"

Saturn gripped Catus roughly and they were suddenly in the atrium of a dark domus. It was quiet and rank, and the only sound was the slow steady drip of water from the roof tiles into the filthy impluvium. The walls were sickly too, their paint peeling away in black moldy curls. All doors were shut, locked tightly, except for the main door onto the street. The place was utterly devoid of objects, no scrap of an iron bracket for a torch in the wall, no brazier, no bronze remaining upon the door where the knocker had been. The place had been robbed, utterly stripped.

"Where are we?" Catus asked Saturn who stood in the shadows with his great scythe leaning against his old muscular shoulder.

Still, Saturn refused to talk, but nodded to a spot before the impluvium where, in the shadows, a rickety table had been laid out.

Catus froze when he saw it, for upon the table there appeared to be a body, covered in a sooty sheet, the sort used by labourers to avoid scuffing floors during their works. The body was small and bony beneath the sheet, and for a moment, Catus wondered if it was a child, but the length was too great for that.

The smell of decay was in the air for no incense burned and no wild flowers had been placed about the body to cover the offensive reek that death brought. Catus approached, the sleeve of his tunic covering his mouth, his eyes wide. He was about to turn away when the sound of voices came onto the scene from the front door.

Catus turned to see four business men in cleaned and pressed togas, other landlords with whom he had regular meetings and negotiations, though he usually fleeced them in their dealings. They certainly were out of place there.

"Cassius? Fabianus? Orban, and Turnus? What are you all doing here?"

As if in answer to his ghostly query, Cassius spoke.

"Funny that we should meet here of all places!"

"Yes indeed. One last meeting," laughed Orban.

"Quite," Turnus added, gazing about the place with distaste. "I would have thought it to be richer here."

"The scavengers have long since done their work," Cassius pointed out. "I only found out when I heard others talking about bidding on his properties."

"Well, I for one," said the one named Fabianus, "I only came to make sure that it was true. That he is truly gone from this world."

They all four looked at the body, their senses only then picking up the odour of death, and in concert they covered their noses as they approached the table lit only by a sliver of moon.

Catus could not see the body for the four men blocked the way as they pulled back the sheet.

"So it's true," Fabianus said with a hint of relief in his voice.

"Good riddance!" said Orban.

"Well," added Turnus. "This really is the best gift for Saturnalia, isn't it?" he laughed. "What are you doing?" he asked Cassius who was leaning over the body.

Cassius, by far the most brazen of the four, had reached down and plucked something from the dead person's mouth. He held up a gold aureus in triumph. "Aha! My own share of the plunder!" he joked.

"The boatman won't have his share if you take that," Orban said, reticence in his voice.

"Oh, don't worry," Cassius said, popping the coin into a leather pouch he gripped tightly in one fist. "He didn't believe in anything. Trust me, the Gods won't give a fig when he shows up!"

"Well, we've confirmed the news," Fabianus said, moving toward the door. "Let's go to be purified of this and then Cassius, you can treat us all to a round with your new-found wealth!"

They left the domus together, closer than they had ever been, hilarity upon their lips and a hearty 'Io Saturnalia!' shouted in the street outside.

Catus wheeled on Saturn. "I had no idea they were so terrible! To rob the dead of their ferry passage! It's unthinkable!"

"Many things that are unthinkable can become reality…"

It was the first time Saturn had spoken, and the sound of it shredded Catus' courage to ribbons. He fell silent, fearful of the voice should it make utterance again. The god's voice sounded like wind and thrashing waves at once, like grinding upon stone or the burning of fire. It was horrible.

But Catus still reeled from what he had just seen and found his own voice, shuddering though it might be.

"Please, oh Saturn, take me from this place of death, for it chills me to my marrow and spirit. I do not want to know who that man behind me in the shadows is, but I would be in a domus where there is some feeling…some…some tenderness to melt the icy cold that I feel enveloping me. I beg you!"

Saturn hefted his scythe and suddenly they were in the top floor apartment of a tenement where a young man in dirty workman's clothes burst in through the door to greet an anxious woman, his wife, holding a crying baby. The man closed the door quickly, waiting to catch his excited, panting breath. He had obviously run hard and fast on some errand.

"Did you find out?" his wife asked, shushing the baby as she bounced continuously. She too wore rags and the child was wrapped in an old blanket. "Is it true?"

The man stood straight from his hunched position where he had caught his breath. His eyes were wild with elation, or perhaps it was madness, but it did not matter on that day, for both were of the same making.

He nodded slowly. "It is," he said, stepping toward her and kissing her on the mouth before kissing his child's head. He laughed nervously for a moment, and then stopped himself. "He's dead, my love," he whispered, and relief washed over her face too. "He's dead! Our troubles are finally at an end. The Gods have smiled on us. He's dead!"

"Who is dead?" Catus asked Saturn again. "They are rejoicing at a man's death! I asked for tenderness!" He turned back to the couple and saw them embracing once more before going to the humble altar they kept and lighting a single candle.

"Io Saturnalia," they whispered together before a chorus of whoops and cheers echoed about the entire tenement block outside.

Though he could not see who yelled without or where they lived, the words they shouted reached Catus' ears as clearly as a market seller on the eve of Saturnalia.

"He is truly dead!" they shouted. "Praise the Gods!"

"Oh Saturn, why do you show me these unfeeling people of little consequence?" Catus asked, immediately regretting the words for all the darkness in the god's stare.

Saturn's fist reached out and grabbed hold of Catus' tunic and a moment later they were once more in the courtyard where Bacchus had shown Catus the celebrations of Giles Amadea and his family and friends.

"Yes…yes," Catus said, nodding as he looked around. "If anywhere in the Suburra will show us a genuine moment of heartfelt tenderness, this is certainly it!"

Saturn looked gravely at Catus and then across the courtyard to the door that belonged to the ground-level home of Giles and his family.

Catus began to walk toward the door but his footsteps slowed when the sound of weeping reached his ears. He turned to the aged god behind him, but Saturn pointed insistently at the door. Catus continued his spectral path through the door and found himself in the main room of Giles' home.

There, he spotted Giles' wife, Marcia, standing at a

table cutting onions with the help of her older boy, Lucian, while, at the end of the table, the older daughter, Diana, cradled her two younger sisters in her arms, singing them a slow and soft lullaby though it was not yet time for bed.

"Giles must be out with little Paulus," Catus said to himself as he watched the family he had seen so joyful at another Saturnalia. "But what is wrong with them?"

Marcia sat, cutting slowly, her eyes full of tears that flowed more than was usual from any onion. Occasionally, Lucian stopped his own cutting and laid his sinewy arm across her back, giving her a comforting squeeze.

"All will be well, Mother," the boy said. "Please don't cry so much."

Marcia took a rag and dried her eyes once more before looking at her boy. "The onions upset me more than usual today," she said, sniffling. "I would be done before your father comes home, and show him what a proper Roman matron I am."

"Oh, Mother…" said Diana, looking with reddened eyes down the table. "Father expects no such thing."

"I know, Love," Marcia said. "But things are different now, and we need our strength if we are to come through the days ahead. Your father so loved Saturnalia."

"And he will again!" Lucian added. "I've never known him not to shout 'Io Saturnalia!' at the top of his voice!"

"That's true!" said both Calida and Callula from their sister's lap.

"There is hope left, Mother, you will see," Lucian said, though his voice shook against his will.

His mother embraced him tightly then, her knife falling to the floorboards just as the door opened.

Catus turned to see Giles Amadea, the former gladiator in his employ, come slowly over the threshold.

And he barely recognized the man.

Giles stood there with a small stained satchel slung over his shoulder, and gazed about the room with shot and watery eyes, the eyes of an old man who is haunted by a lifetime of tragedy.

Immediately, Marcia stood from the table and went to him, her arms wrapped tightly about him as they held each other for a few moments as if in the eye of a great storm.

Then the children all gathered around them and added to the warmth of that family unity. Giles closed his eyes and two streams of withheld sorrow ran down upon the heads of his younger children...all save one.

"We were worried about you," Marcia said. "Saturnalia eve and you've been gone for hours."

"Always a hard worker, you are, Giles!" Catus said, his words inconsequential.

Giles went across the room to the small lararium where a small wooden statue of Saturn stood, and from the satchel he produced a candle which he lit and stood beside the god's image. He bent his head and mouthed a silent prayer before turning back to his family.

Catus noticed the dark circles beneath Giles' eyes, the shrunken, depressed body that had replaced the strong, virile and lively body of the gladiator he had been on and off the sand. This was not the man he had seen standing before all the neighbours previously.

"I'm sorry," Giles said rubbing his eyes and making a very great effort to stand straight. "I went to speak with one of the minor pontifs about the right locus religiosus in the necropolis."

They were all silent, and Lucian and Diana made a sign against ill-omen.

"No," he said to the two older children. "There is no need to worry. I went to see it."

"You did?" Marcia asked.

"Yes. I couldn't help myself. My feet wandered for miles until I got there." He took a deep breath. "It's a beautiful, peaceful place. And there were hundreds of other children there. The cypress trees are ancient and reach to the sky, so dark and green, and there is a wondrous view of the stars from there, away from the lights of the city."

Giles seemed then to stare off into another place and time, and so they all did, imagining as they were the scene he had described.

"Where is little Paulus?" Catus asked, an unfamiliar panic and pang in his chest. He looked about the room and then toward the door, but none there expected another.

There was a void to swallow the world whole.

Giles took a deep breath and kissed each of those gathered around him before reaching back into his satchel and pulling out another candle which he lit from the previous one. Silently, Giles went down the central path of the small domus where darkness hung heavy, cut only by the singular flame he carried.

Catus followed him past the red and blue curtains of the few cubicula until, out of the darkness emerged a tiny face wreathed in raven hair. "Paulus?" Catus gasped, remembering the young boy he had seen standing beside his father among so many friends and neighbours.

Giles' candle shed its light upon the little body of his son, laid out in his best tunic and surrounded by flowers and fragrant herbs.

Catus wanted to place his hand upon the shuddering shoulders of the grieving man before him, to speak some words of comfort to him that the Gods were indeed real, and that they would care for his son in the Afterlife. But he was unable to help in his current state, no more than the air about them could provide comfort at a time such as that.

"My little boy…" Giles said, weeping silently into his fists after setting the candle down in a bowl of sand beside the small table where his son was laid out. "I miss you. How shall I ever manage without you in my life?"

More tears… More anguish… Enough to rip the heart out of any man, no matter how hard his soul.

And Catus crumpled beneath the grief he felt radiating off of Giles - the loss of a kindly child…of a sister long gone…of a love lost forever…

"I am sorry, my Paulus… I'm sorry for not having given you a better life. I would have taken your place. There are many children where you will go tomorrow…and you'll be able to finally play with them all. You'll run, and jump, and dive in the sea just like you always wanted to." Giles hung his head and sniffed as he reached into his satchel and pulled out a pouch. He unlaced it and tipped out a single silver denarius. "Gods," he said as he placed the coin in his son's mouth. "Please see him safely to Elysium. Give us all strength and hope such as his…my tiny boy…"

Giles wept again, leaning upon the table and resting his face upon the little, still chest of his son. He kissed his tiny face again, and brushed the dark hair back from his closed eyes. Then he stood, took up the candle, and went back to his family, drying his eyes as he went.

Marcia came immediately to his arms and he smiled at her, an act that would have required as much courage as facing down a charge of Parthian cavalry.

"I'm fine," he said to his wife and children. "We are, it should be said, blessed by Fortuna that we should have known him at all, and been so blessed to have called him family."

They were all nodding as he spoke, not a dry eye

amongst them, though they each smiled at their own happy memories of Paulus Amadea.

"And his kindness is played out in the words of all who knew him," Giles continued. "Why, this very evening on my way back from...from..." He caught himself before another wave of grief overtook him. "I was met by Julian Corbin, the kindly nephew of Catus Pompilius. He asked me what was wrong, as I seemed not myself, and I told him of little Paulus." Giles looked into his wife's eyes. "He wept at the news I gave him... Our son touched so many, and he didn't even know it. Julian offered, in genuine kindness, if there was anything he could do to help. I said no, but thanked him. But still, he thrust a denarius into my hand and insisted that I use it for what good it could bring. He reiterated his sympathies and his offer of help and told me that tomorrow he would offer prayers to our Paulus in the temple of Jupiter, Juno and Minerva."

The family's eyes were wide with wonder at this kindness and they all knew that despite all the grief they felt in that moment, there was still goodness and hope in the world, no matter how dark it seemed. And they smiled and held each other up once more with the fond memories of love and faith they carried with them.

May the Gods bless such mortals as Paulus Amadea!

Catus watched them and then turned to Saturn who had entered the front door of the small domus.

"I see now, oh dread Saturn... I asked for kindness and feeling, and you have shown it to me. I am ready to go back to my own home."

Saturn smiled grimly then and held out his hand to Catus.

Catus reached out to the god's grasp and the room spun dizzyingly out of sight.

Bitter wind and sea spray battered Catus' face where he stood. A great howling rushed all about him and a crash of waves shook the rock beneath his feet.

Catus opened his eyes and saw that he stood not in his domus on the Esquiline Hill of Rome, but rather on a remote, rocky and wild cliffside promontory overlooking a raging sea. A red sun dipped into the western horizon and dark clouds scoured the sky to the East. But it was the great maw of a cave before him that concerned Catus in that moment of terror.

"Where are we?" he asked Saturn.

The god stood taller than he had been, now behind Catus, his great scythe arcing over his white head, dripping with silvery sea water.

"This isn't Rome!" Catus yelled above the howl of the wind about the mouth of that dreadful cave.

Saturn shook his head and lunged forward to push Catus into that gaping black abyss.

The mortal man screamed as he fell farther and farther into the earth until all went black as death itself...

He felt his body bruised, and pain radiated up and down his limbs, but Catus kept his eyes shut for fear of what might meet them. For a few moments, he hoped it had been a dream, a horrible, desolate dream from which he could now wake and set about the things he had been mulling over.

He listened, but all he could hear was the wind, and some distant whispers.

"Rise...Catus Pompilius!" that dreaded voice said, clearer now, but still reminiscent of grinding rock and waves.

Catus felt his hopes plummet. He sat up on his knees, then opened his eyes.

Saturn stood beside him, vibrant…alive…godly. He shone with a radiance that Catus had not seen before, but it was not as a light of hope. No. It was something grave, severe.

Squinting, Catus Pompilius looked around. Before him was a softly-flowing river of dark water, the sound of which trickled into his mind, tempting him with thirst. He turned to see a far distant desert, a grey and ashen wasteland he did not remember passing through. Beside him was a wide road of black, though the material of it was not obvious to Catus who thought it to be some kind of fine rock, perhaps of adamant.

Saturn stood upon this roadway which was not visible beyond the river. He pointed at the riverbank before Catus and a two-handled, golden cup. "Drink of the water of Lethe."

Catus recoiled, terror gripping his heart in an iron fist then, as he knew the name of one of the Underworld's waters. "Must I?" he begged…pleaded upon his knees.

"Drink!" Saturn commanded.

With a shaking hand, Catus reached out for the brilliant cup and dipped it in the water. His hand paused with the rim nearly upon his lips, hoping the god would stop him, but no word was said.

Catus drank.

In that moment, as the cool water slid down his throat, he felt a wave of emptiness spread like a poison throughout his very soul. The helplessness was overwhelming and he felt like weeping for all that he had squandered and lost, the time he had wasted, which he was now robbed of by the Gods themselves.

"Come with me now," Saturn said, hefting his scythe and turning to face down the black road and a bridge of grey stone arching over the river.

Catus followed, his feet shuffling upon the black path as he was led over the river Lethe, and as soon as they had crossed to the other side, another land spread out into the distance before them and to both sides.

They were in vast meadows of green and white flowers as far as Catus' aged eyes could see, and as they went, the faint forms of as many people as there are stars in the sky appeared among those ghostly-white petals.

Catus observed those he could see up close, those clinging to the black thread of the road and went inexorably onward, seemingly into infinity. Their faces were emotionless masks as they wandered together, yet ignorant of each other in their passing. He noted that their only desire was for the flowers.

"What are these fields…these flowers?" Catus asked.

"These are the Meadows of Asphodel," Saturn said. "The souls who dwell here led unremarkable lives, lives that did not catch the attention of the Gods, that did nothing to make an impression on time itself." Saturn spoke as he walked onward, never looking back, never pausing for the mortal man in tow.

Catus looked at some of the souls who knelt before the tall stalks of those ghostly blooms and saw them reach out to stroke them, their hands pulling back in pain and covered with blood that appeared to leach from the base of each flower. But despite the pain, they insisted on touching again, and again, until their clothes were reddened beyond reckoning.

"Am…am I to stay here?" Catus asked, horrified as he watched the souls.

"No. The Meadows are not for you, Catus Pompilius," Saturn said, glancing over his shoulder for the first time since they had begun that long walk.

"Where are we going then?" Catus asked, but Saturn did not answer.

They walked on, and it might have been an eternity with the clouds moving unnaturally at speed in the iron grey skies, and the cold light of the sun and moon rising and diving over their heads.

Catus felt as though he left pieces of himself along the road, his mind weary, and his heart - what remained of it - tattered and worn.

They walked and walked along that road until they came to another clear river and a bridge. The bridge arched steeply over the waters, and at the top, Catus chanced a look down.

"What are those forms in the water?" he asked, unable to help himself.

"The Dead," Saturn said.

And in that moment Catus noticed the flow of pale faces and blank eyes of thousands upon thousands of women and men, their hair like seaweed in a current as they washed to the distant horizon.

They reached the other side of the bridge and the sound of weeping and wailing exploded in Catus' ears, heart-wrenching pain, the noise of desperate loss and misunderstanding.

"Why do they weep so?" Catus asked. The green fields of that land stretched even farther into the distance, so far that he thought they might run off the edges of the world. In some places he spied gleaming forms of queens or kings sitting high above the others upon thrones of gold beset with glinting jewels and mounds of food and pitchers of wine. But the kings and queens upon those lonely mounds neither ate or drank or raised their heads to look at those milling around them.

"We pass now through the Mourning Fields, Catus Pompilius," Saturn said. "Here dwell those sad and desperate souls who loved and were never loved in return. They wanted with all their being to give themselves to another, but their sad love was unrequited. They did not exist for others, and it was their downfall that it was so."

Catus stopped and gazed upon the faces of the men and women weeping into the distance. The sight gave him great sadness, but he knew it was no sadness compared with what those poor beings felt, and would feel, for all eternity.

He closed his eyes as he walked on after the tall, red-cloaked form of Saturn. On and on they went.

The road stretched for an age until it came to a titanic range - no, a wall! - of snow-capped mountains, and a tunnel that cut through them.

Catus already felt himself utterly defeated after the eternal walk through the previous meadows and fields of the Underworld, for make no mistake, he now knew that was where he was. But upon seeing the great mountains rising up before his insignificant self, and hearing the cries of those souls who attempted to clamber up those rocky heights only to tumble to a second death, he now felt desperation beyond reckoning, utter and complete helplessness.

Saturn continued before him, heading into the darkness of the tunnel through the mountains.

Catus followed him, if only to tear his gaze away from the souls lacerating themselves upon the rock faces to either side. He went into the darkness, led only by the cold glow of Saturn's scythe. The darkness gave him long moments of thought and fright, of what he could have done better in the life the Gods had granted him, and what might await him on the other side of the darkness.

"Walk on, Catus Pompilius!" Saturn's voice shot back in the pitch darkness as he trod the road ever onward.

Catus was ready to lie down upon the black earth and let himself die, then and there, with the images and faces that had gone before, all he had wasted beyond repair. He was prepared to let the god strike him down and was about to speak as much when, what did he see, but sunlight!

Oh, sunlight, brilliant and warm!

The jaws of that tunnel opened to spit him out into a world he had never believed possible, nor ever simply believed in!

Elysium.

Either side of the black road, for hundreds, no thousands, of miles, a great green land lush in trees, streams, and brimming with life, stretched out with welcoming views. It was a panorama of hope, and for a moment, Catus began to hope that this now was his new home.

He sought out the men and women who peopled it, and noted their great, shining beauty, the perfection of their shape and form, the music they sang, and the feats they performed. Some heroes sped across the grassy plains in chariots drawn by magical horses, while in the clear blue skies above, winged stallions swept and dove. In glades of emerald oaks, demigods gathered to sing and dine, to drink and tell tales of their glorious pasts. Within the walls of gilded and marble palaces, heroes enjoyed the afterlife of their labours.

All around Catus, he spied those who could only have been heroes or gods, and not a few of them he believed he recognized, not of sight, but out of the tales of their deeds performed in the mortal world.

"Can they ever leave here?" he asked Saturn, catching up to the god.

"No. But they live in eternal contentment with the lives they led and the names they have left behind." Saturn stopped and looked down upon Catus. "I wonder what the mortal world will remember of Catus Pompilius?"

Catus said nothing, but in truth, he had been thinking that very same thing, and he felt shame and insignificance as he looked around that world of wonder, so much so that he walked more quickly and closer to Saturn than he had previously dared.

The road went on through the Elysian fields, lands of beauty and wonder they seemed, one after another, utopian worlds in microcosm. Nowhere, as far as his seeking eyes could gather, did Catus see dismay or unhappiness, discord or strife. It was as if those joyous beings had fought long, hard-suffering lives for this singular victory in death. And they regretted none of it.

As night fell swiftly, fires burned into the distance of those fields, a star-pocked land.

"What are those fires appearing?" Catus asked as

the light began to return.

"Even in Elysium, the altars of the Gods are not absent sacrifice," Saturn said as a thick mist enveloped them.

Catus clung to the dark form of Saturn, his red cloak only just visible. Then the lapping of water could be heard and the black road stopped.

They stood upon a dock, and there before them was a broad black river.

It chilled Catus to look upon those dark waters, for they could be none other than the river of death itself, the Styx.

Saturn walked to the end of the dock, the black water lapping thickly about the pylons, until they came to the end where the form of a barge emerged.

Catus swallowed hard, trying to muster a prayer in his fear, but he froze as his eyes followed the length of the skull-encrusted barge of black wood until, at the stern the tall cloaked figure of Acheron himself observed him, his mottled, long-fingered hand extended for his payment.

There were cries of terror across the water, and the howl of harpies somewhere in the mist.

"Pay him," Saturn ordered.

Catus fumbled in his tunic and found he had no coin, not even a single bronze as to pay the ferryman.

Saturn loomed over him, the great blade of the scythe seeming to bend toward him with an aspect of death.

"I...I...I don't have any...forgive me, please!" he said, looking at the boatman and then shutting his eyes immediately in terror as those dark and sunken sockets gazed back in anger.

Just then, Catus felt something tugging at the back of his tunic. He shrieked and turned, and there, standing before him was a young boy.

Catus wept when he saw him, for it was young Paulus Amadea.

The shade smiled at Catus and reached out for his hand.

Catus let it take his hand and felt something deposited there.

"Carry on, Catus Pompilius," the shade said, smiling up at him. Even in death, the boy was a blessing indeed.

"I…I… You should not be here," Catus mumbled.

The shade smiled again. "All is well. You must go now." The boy then nodded, turned, and walked back into the mist.

"Wait, little Paulus!" Catus cried, holding the single silver coin in his trembling hand. "Wait…"

But the boy was gone.

Catus turned and went to the edge of the dock. He handed the coin to Acheron, and stepped aboard to sit opposite Saturn.

A horn blew in the misty air, and the barge sailed away as Acheron set about his labour of ferrying them across.

The journey did not take long, but Catus wished it had, for it delayed his meeting whatever lay ahead.

After a short while upon the sad waters, the crossing was complete and the barge pulled up beneath the branches of a pomegranate tree sprouting out of the solid rock of a hewn pier.

"Out," Saturn said, stepping off the barge and beginning to walk again.

Catus clambered after him until they came to a

titanic staircase that led up the side of a mountain of black adamant. The mountain shook there, and the air was rent by screams and cries. Swarming the air of those heights far above, Catus could see winged beasts with, he believed, the faces of women, and as they swooped toward him, the faces took on the visages of people he had had dealings with in the mortal world. Every face was pained and full of anger, and were he not dead, as he was now starting to believe, he knew they would have haunted him all the rest of his days.

They reached the top of the megalithic staircase and stepped onto a broad smooth circle of stone. Catus turned, his chest heaving, and looked out across the Underworld to see the black road stretching into infinity, across each of the realms they had passed through.

"Catus Pompilius!" a great voice charged, and the mountain shook.

Saturn took hold of Catus a second later and dragged him to the centre of the circular space.

Catus fell to his hands and knees and stared at the ground.

"Look up." The voice was harsh and unforgiving, and each syllable carried a hundred thousand possible deaths and torments.

Catus' head shook as he looked up from his prostrate position, sweat and tears pouring down his deeply creased brow and face.

There, upon a deep purple throne of stone, carved with ancient writing not known to man, sat Dis himself, Lord of the Underworld. The god was tall, and robed all in black which contrasted with his pale, almost translucent skin. His hair was long and oily and raven black, and it clung to his godly features.

But it was the eyes of Dis that struck terror into Catus then. They burned bright with fury, pitiless, merciless, unyielding in the judgement they now sought to visit upon the mortal kneeling before him. To either side of him stood radiant and unhappy goddesses, and up the mountainside, fiery and jaundiced eyes stared in his direction, ready to do his bidding at a moment.

To the side, Saturn stood sentry, his scythe resting upon the ground now, both his hands gripping the haft easily.

"I have been expecting you, Catus Pompilius," Dis said, his voice a dreadful note resounding upon the mountain. "You know your crimes and the weight of that shrivelled heart in your chest. So much misery… So much greed…" Dis shook his head, but smiled as he gazed toward a descending staircase to Catus' right.

Horrible screams tore up those stairs, anguish beyond imagining, eternal and unbending. He looked back at Catus. "Do you know why you stand before me?"

Catus' head spun and his senses revolted. He was unable to answer, to move, to shrug even. He only shook his head.

"Your judgement falls to me, mortal man. Your peril."

"P...p...p...please," Catus managed. "I know all that I have done. And I...I...beg for forgiveness. Please!"

"Beg!" Dis stood suddenly and it seemed his head soared into the sky as he gazed down on Catus as if he were an insect. "How many begged forgiveness of you and were denied? I should have my harpies tear out your tongue for uttering the word!"

"No! Please!" Catus said, unable to stop himself. He looked around for a place to run and saw to his left an ascending staircase brilliant with golden light. Like a beacon in the darkness it called to him.

Dis laughed. "You do not think the Isle of the Blessed is for such as you?" The god shook his head. "I sit in judgement here, at the bottom of the world, for all mortals. You..." his great pale hand pointed directly at

Catus and it was like a spear thrust. "You shall not escape torment, nor see the world of men again."

In that moment, more cries cracked the air from the staircase to the right, and Catus trembled for it could only have been Tartarus itself to which Dis now pointed.

"No…" Catus cried. "I beg you," he said to Saturn. "I shall make sacrifice the whole of my days, oh great god Saturn. Please!"

Saturn stepped aside and from behind him stepped three hideous creatures, each of them eyeing Catus, slavering as they looked upon him.

Furies.

Yes, they were his, just as the shade of Krelis Manvilio had been tormented by his own, these were, Catus knew it in his gut, to be his own eternal companions.

The furies had the likeness of women but they were possessed of wrecked bodies with long claws, fangs, and the spread of bat-like wings that flapped from their backs. They howled and hissed as they circled Catus, and their clawed hands slashed out to rake his back.

Catus screamed out as he twisted and turned to avoid them, but they were persistent, as forever they would be.

As the furies circled, they hissed words at him, laughing, revelling in it. "Ignorance!!! Want!!!" They said, now dancing and floating about him, their laughter joined by Dis himself from upon his throne. "Hate!!! Greed!!!"

"Oh, Catus Pompilius!" Dis said, standing now and looking down upon the furies as they circled their charge. "Look where your faithlessness has brought you. A fortune of pain and suffering!" he laughed and pointed at the dark path of descent into Tartarus. "Down there you will see others who have been brought low by their supreme arrogance, their hubris. And if you like, you may dine with the Dead at Saturnalia! Though they may feast upon you first!" Dis nodded his hoary head, and the furies pushed Catus toward the stairs.

But he fought them, desperate, strength in his limbs like he had never experienced. The furies clawed and cut at him, their teeth gnashing, but still he fought them, making his way to kneel before Saturn, gripping his blood-red robe in his fists.

"Oh, great Saturn! I know that the course of my life has led me to this future! I know that if I were to remain unchanged in life, in my very heart and nature, that I would be deserving of the eternal torments of Tartarus for all the cruelty and harm that I have done. I know it!" Catus bowed, tears pouring down his face, but he continued, looking up at the god. "But if I were to leave the path my life was set upon…to meet my fellow mortals with kindness, and to give the Gods their due…surely this future would also change, and my fate would not be this?"

Catus Pompilius shook, still gripping Saturn's robe. "I know now that I am the one whose death brought so much joy to so many in Rome. I know it!" he wept. "But I will change, and become a man the world will weep to lose for all the good he has done. I will make sacrifice to you not only at Saturnalia but all the days of my life to honour the joy you have always brought to the world. Please, oh great Saturn! Please!"

The god looked down upon Catus and for the first time, there was pity in his eternal eyes, and they grew as bright as the constellation of cerei that burned for him in every home and temple and public place.

But the furies pulled Catus away, and he screamed, that mortal man. He realized then that all was lost, that he would never have the chance to right the wrongs he had already begun to imagine in his mind.

The descent to horrific darkness loomed like the

gorge of some terrible beast.

Then Saturn walked quickly, and the great scythe swung back as he twisted to strike.

Catus screamed again as the arcing blade flashed toward him and sent him into the depts of Tartarus, a chorus of wailing and despair echoing above his own cries.

And he fell!

VI

THE WORLD

He fell to the floor... His floor! Catus Pompilius groaned, his face wet with tears, his body shaking with terror and sadness.

But then his ears heard not the torment and screaming of fell Tartarus, but rather the dark quiet of his own domus. He opened his flooded eyes to see a single ray of light bursting in through the window of his own cubiculum.

"What?" He touched the floor, his couch, the table. He ran his hands over his face and head, felt at his back for horrific wounds, and felt nothing wrong. He was home...home...and more importantly, he was alive!

Catus fumbled toward the window at the back of his cubiculum and threw open the shutters only to be blinded by a brilliant morning assault of sunshine. He shut his eyes tight for the burning it caused his lids, but he stood there, feeling the heat, the light covering his entire sobbing body.

"I'm alive!" he yelled. "Oh, all you Gods…I thank you!" He was so overcome with emotion that he wept openly then, his entire person convulsing in mingled grief and joy, relief and hope yet to be held onto. He opened his eyes and gazed out at the villa walls of his neighbours, and then beyond to the packed rooftops of the Suburra, beyond to the Palatine and Capitoline Hills of that blessed, imperial city.

He then jumped up. Yes, jumped! And danced around his cubiculum like a drunk who has been through an entire amphora of fine Falernian. In truth he danced and jumped like a man who has been granted a second chance at life, a gift not given to many mortals.

Catus Pompilius thought of all he had seen and heard…felt…that night, by the Gods' grace, and he fell once more to his knees at the window in a pool of morning light. He raised his hands fervently to the heavens above.

"Oh, great Saturn…oh Bacchus…oh divine goddess, Vesta…with all my heart, thank you for this. I will make right the wrongs I have done! I will, from this day for the length of all my days, be a man of goodness and honour as you have taught me this night, for I know now that what pleases the divine only serves to better the world. I will never forget to sacrifice to each of you for as long as there is life in me!" he said, so quickly that he panted, but he meant every syllable of what he said, and felt it too. Never was a man more in earnest than Catus Pompilius in that moment, for now, he believed and trusted in the Gods.

He stood then, shaking, but pushing himself on with the thought of all that he wanted to do that day and every day. He began to rush from the room, but paused in his excitement one more time as he remembered his old partner, Krelis, and spared a thought for him who suffered for them both.

"Krelis…my friend. I thank you too…and I won't forget this…" After a moment, he jumped up, clapping his hands and was out of the cubiculum like a child, rushing down the cracking marble of the staircase to the peristylium below.

"Woohoo!" he yelled, his voice echoing throughout the dark domus. "Yip! Yip!" he cried as he skipped across the dead garden toward the lararium. Inside, he shook his head at what had been done to it, and imagined fresh paint, statues of the Gods, and a fire burning brightly day and night flanked by cerei for Saturnalia and all the days of the year. "Oh, Vesta, I will bring your sacred light into this domus, I swear it!"

For a moment, he thought he spied the divine goddess standing in the shadows there, and he bowed though it may only have been to the darkness. However, he doubted it, for he felt her presence everywhere, all around him, all three of them and more watching over him and filling Rome with life.

Then, he panicked...

"What day is it? Have I missed it?"

Catus Pompilius rushed from the lararium and across the garden, and through the atrium to unbolt the front door which he threw open. He fell into the street laughing and panicking all at once, until he grabbed hold of a group of youths passing by laughing and singing bawdy songs.

"Ho, you there!" he called.

"Easy, grandfather!" one of them said. "Slow down now!"

"No! I won't!" Catus retorted. "What day is it?"

"What's he on about?" asked one of the fellows.

"I said, what day is it, young man?" Catus replied to the first.

"Why, it's the first day of Saturnalia, grandfather! We're on our way to the Forum for the great sacrifice and feast."

"It's today?" Catus asked again, incredulous.

"Yes!" the young man said, laughing, unable to help himself seeing this delirious Esquiline resident so unaware and excited.

"That's wonderful!" Catus called. "Io Saturnalia!" and that at the top of his voice.

"Io Saturnalia!" the group called back to him before heading off to the Forum.

Catus turned. "There's so much to do!" He spun around, taking in the world as if for the first time, and there spotted a wagon coming from the other side of the hill, a wagon filled with boar, and cages of chickens, and row upon row of suckling pigs. "You there! Stop!"

The wagon driver and his sons looked suspiciously at the old man in the street, but stopped nonetheless for they were on the Esquiline, and that was usually safe for passage.

"What?" asked the farmer, looking down at Catus.

"How much for your entire wagon of goods?" Catus asked.

The farmer had little to say to that, but looked to his sons who shrugged their shoulders, for never had anyone ever asked such a ridiculous question.

"Too much, sir," the man said. "We're on our way to Trajan's forum to sell our goods. What need have you for so much?"

"Oh, my need is great, and so is that of a great many others. How much?" Catus asked again. "Plus the delivery of it all to various tenements about the city."

The farmer whispered to his sons, and there was a bit of back and forth, until finally the largest of the sons jumped down and whispered it in Catus' ear.

Catus clapped his hands. "Done!"

The farmer's eyes were wide with disbelief, but he nodded dumbly and motioned for his son to follow Catus inside.

"Now, I'm going to give you a list of all the tenements where these are to be delivered..." Catus said quickly as he went into his tablinum to count out not a few denarii and aurea. "I want no one to know who has sent these delectables to them, but only that it is one who seeks to wish them well upon Saturnalia, and wants them well-fed!" he laughed.

"Very good, sir," the young man said. "We can

make sure everyone gets a portion. We can even help'em set them to roasting!"

"Perfect!" Catus exclaimed. "And I want that great boar to be delivered to the family of Giles Amadea at the first tenement on this list!" He handed a paper to the young man. "They above all must have a full meal from this. Understood?"

"Yes, sir!"

"And if you carry out your duty to me as I outline, you and your brothers and father must return here on your way home and I'll give you another quarter of the price I'm paying you for your goods and service!" Catus tossed him a purse heavy with coin which thumped on the young man's chest.

He stared at Catus and nodded slowly. "We'll do that, sir. You can trust us."

"Oh, I do, lad! I do!" Catus said, going back out with him to the wagon.

The young man jumped up into the wagon and quickly told his father what was agreed. The older man looked down at Catus and removed his pileus which he was wearing in honour of Saturnalia. He then turned in his seat, took one of the finest suckling pigs from the rack, and handed it down to Catus who took it.

"Io Saturnalia!" Catus said, holding the trophy of kindness aloft.

"Io Saturnalia!" the father and sons yelled back as they carried on down the road toward the first tenement on the list.

Catus watched them go and turned to see several of his neighbours and their slaves staring gawp-eyed at him.

"Io Saturnalia, good citizens!" he called, a smile spread across his face.

Not many answered for all the shock they felt in that absurd moment, but others, once attuned, shouted the greeting back as Catus jumped toward his door and paused to kiss the gorgon-headed knocker upon the solid plane of the door. "Ha!" he cried as he went in to prepare himself.

"Dominus?"

There, in the middle of the atrium, was Ida. She stood there, her eyes wide in confusion and not a little terror for the apparition of jollity before her. In fact, the sight of her master skipping in at the door, swinging a suckling pig and smiling from ear to ear, humming even, set her in such a shock that she nearly fell over.

"Oh, Ida! Isn't it a wonderful day?" Catus

exclaimed to her, dancing around her like a lunatic Bacchante. "Io Saturnalia!" he said. "Today is a big day, Ida! The Gods have blessed us. I want you to cook this!" He handed her the pig. "And you are to make as much bread as you wish until the entire domus smells of its baking. I'll also need my clean toga, if I have one!" Then he stopped himself. "No! Just tell me where, and I shall do the rest, for today of all days, you should not work, but rest. Enjoy life, and living!"

Ida stood there still, shaking and looking around as if for a route of escape. But then her fear subsided and she looked upon her old dominus.

"Dominus? What has happened?"

Catus stopped in front of her. Then he calmed, and was in earnest. "Oh, Ida… So much has happened…so much. But I haven't time to explain. I must…" He looked upon her solidly for a few uncomfortable seconds, and then began nodding vigorously. "Yes. That's it!"

"What, Dominus?"

"I'm off to the baths, but when I get back you shall know the truth of what has happened. But let me tell you now, Ida. This domus shall be bright and warm at last, I swear it! I am going to hire the finest workers to rebuild and paint, and it shall be a place of joy and light and laughter such as you or I have never seen."

"Yes, Dominus," she said, and Catus laughed at how he must look to her.

"I'll return in a while!" he said before rushing from the atrium and leaving her standing there holding the pig. He paused briefly over the spot where Krelis had fallen seven years past, and spared a thought for the shade who had struck such terror into him and yet offered him so much hope.

Ida watched Catus Pompilius go upstairs and she wondered if the Gods had finally had their crack at him.

It was a joy to be out in Rome on that sunny winter morning as Catus Pompilius strode through the streets smiling and casting a jolly 'Io Saturnalia!' at anyone who would listen. He was a new man in constant wonder of everything he saw, as if the world had opened up to him for the very first time from behind a dark veil.

Everywhere he looked there was colour and joy and hilarity in people's faces, everywhere he listened there was music and song, laughter betwixt friends and even enemies. Saturnalia was in every man, woman, child and animal! It was there in every green garland of holly and ivy hung from every column, and every colourful wall. Even the graffiti that was everywhere came to joyous life before his eyes.

In the shadow of the Colosseum, Catus noted in the crowds that master and slave walked together as equals everywhere, laughing, talking, with even the slaves dressed for merriment and taking a good-natured shot at their masters now and again, all in good fun.

Other groups had already got down to the serious business of gambling with dice and knucklebones, and an urge suddenly came upon Catus to throw! He stepped up to a goodly group of fellows and asked to join for a round.

"Surely, grandfather!" they said, making space.

Catus waited for a turn, and tossed his set amount of coin into the circle. When he was given the dice, he breathed a wish of joy upon them and let the dice fall from his hand.

"The Venus throw!" the group exclaimed.

"Is that good?" Catus asked.

They all looked at each other and laughed. "Of course it is, grandfather! You win!"

"Io Saturnalia!" Catus howled, his face red and

laughing. "You keep my winnings, boys! My gift to you this fine day!" he said, standing up and leaving.

"Io Saturnalia!" they returned as he waived back at them.

Catus had left with a heavy purse which he fully intended to lighten, but first, he wanted to ensure his presence at the great sacrifice at the temple of Saturn.

He made his way through the thickening crowds, along the Via Sacra of the Forum Romanum.

People were everywhere, surrounding the tables that had been set out for the convivium publicum. They gathered in the shadow of the arch of Titus, and upon the steps of the temple of Antoninus and Faustina. They milled around the temple of Vesta, and that of the Divine Julius. Everywhere a person could stand or sit, they did so, right the way up to the Curia, the newly-unveiled arch of Septimius Severus, and the temple of Mars Ultor.

Catus walked until he was at the very end, standing near the Rostra and gazing up at the steps of the temple. There, at the top of the steps, the priest of Saturn held his arms to the sky, his head uncovered.

The crowd grew solemn as it watched, as if with a single purpose for silence, and the entire Forum grew still and reverential.

Catus too felt it as the tibicen beside the priest began to play upon his flute to cover any signs of ill-omen as the victimarius approached with the sacrificial pig. The animal was still as it carried out its sacred duty, the grains of mola salsa falling over its head before the knife flashed and blood was offered up to Saturn upon the altar.

Catus could not hear what words the priest uttered, but he could certainly feel them, as did everyone there. It was as good a sacrifice as any for Rome, and as the smoke began to rise from the flames for the feast, the air exploded with joyful resonance.

From out of the temple came the likeness of Saturn upon his couch, carried by six stout and smiling men, into the Forum to be set upon the Rostra to join in and watch over the proceedings.

Catus continued to gaze toward the temple and there, as everyone else began to make their way to the tables, and any other available space for the banquet, he saw a flickering of the god himself.

Saturn stood beneath the temple's entrance, looking out over the crowd of well-wishers and worshipers, and his eyes fell directly upon Catus Pompilius.

But Catus was no longer afraid. He was inspired! He gazed back at the god from the midst of the crowd, and bowed his head, hand upon his heart.

Saturn nodded, and for anyone else who might have been so blessed to have seen him, it would have been noticed that the god too, had joy, and shared in it. It could be said that the joy and goodwill that spread through Rome from that day, and for the next seven, may well have been due to the best sacrificium ever offered.

Saturn vanished from Catus' sight then, and the old man turned to go, but not before a young child handed him a loaf of steaming bread from a basket she carried around. He ate it with absolute relish, for it was the best bread he had ever eaten. He left the Forum then, leaving the people to their feast beneath a blue winter sky, and made his way to the markets of Trajan as quickly as he could before all the merchandise was gone.

Once there, his mind spun with all that he wanted to get and the prospect of how he would carry it all home.

At the sigillaria sellers' row, Catus purchased the best bees wax cerei to light every room of his domus and to give to anyone he might see or plan on visiting, to their great future shock surely! He filled a sack with carved wooden toys for children in the tenements, handfuls of dice, writing tablets, pipes, perfumes from the East, ivory combs, lamps and more!

It came to the point where a small retinue of boys had been hired to help him carry everything, and they did not dare run off with the loot they carried, for he had promised them ample recompense for their help. Besides, the joy that old man spread with his wonder as he went was absolutely contagious and not a single person who felt it would have considered doing wrong then.

Catus bought cheeses and meats, dates and wine to be consumed at leisure, an entirely new concept to him! When he came to a stall selling what must have been the most explosively coloured synthesis, he asked his group of helpers to stop and aid him in choosing. There was much laughter and pointing and he settled on a great, warm patchwork of yellow, purple, orange, and red. Upon it there were stripes and circles and acanthus leaf patterns. And what would it have been without the matching pileus to top it off? His bald pate had never felt so warm as in the moment that pointed cap was placed upon it, and a cheer rose up!

Wearing his new Saturnalian regalia, the procession continued its progress until Catus stopped suddenly at a seller of women's clothing and looked upon the lovely array of soft silks and colourful wools, cloaks and sandals. He asked his group to wait as he went inside and spoke with the husband and wife sellers about what he needed and for whom.

They nodded, most willing to help him choose, and oh, the woman had most excellent taste, and knew the style that would suit.

The bundle of that most shocking of all gifts tucked carefully beneath his arm, Catus then set off for the Esquiline Hill and home. As he came to the edge of the Suburra, Catus Pompilius called out to two men he saw walking, obviously trying to avoid him.

"Misters Castor and Pollux!" Catus waved, and called a second time. "Io Saturnalia to you!"

The men carried on walking, but Catus was so persistent and loud in his exclamation that they could not help but stop and speak with him.

"What is it, Catus Pompilius?" they asked together.

Catus stepped forward so that he was apart from those following him. He had a task ahead of him in that moment, and he wanted to ensure its completion.

"Good men…" he began, his head bowed slightly, hands clasped before him. "I must apologize to you for my behaviour the other day."

"Yesterday, you mean?" Pollux said.

"Oh, ah, yes. Yesterday." Catus nodded and stopped himself from moving, only looking them directly and earnestly in the eyes. "I was wrong, and I must beg your pardon for the viciousness of my response to your work."

"You were wrong?" Castor asked, seeking confirmation that he was not being had over.

"Yes." Catus nodded, his head higher, lighter that he was able to admit fault. "The work you two gentlemen are doing for the Suburra is…well…more than I have ever done in the entirety of my life. I wish to make it up to you by giving you a donation…a…a sum to aid you in your work this Saturnalia festival and all the year."

The two men looked confused for a moment, but then they smiled as broadly as any man in Rome that day, for their trust in that sacred time of year was surely no longer misplaced, as they thought it had been the day before when the man before them had torn their hopes to ribbons.

Catus leaned forward to whisper to them both. "Sirs, I wish to donate a talent of silver to the betterment of the Suburra and the lives of all the families who dwell there. Not only those in my own tenements, for I will endeavour to aid them anyway, but for all the people of that part of Rome that needs it most. What say you? Can you accept aid from such as myself?"

Catus worried for a moment that they would refuse his help, as well they would be within their rights to do so after his behaviour.

But Castor and Pollux both grasped his hands heartily and asked that the Gods bless Catus Pompilius then and forevermore for his generosity. They promised to come to his domus the very next day as instructed by him.

A song was struck up then as the boys, weighed down with their jolly burdens, paraded Catus Pompilius up the slope of the Esquiline like Emperor Severus might have done on the day of his triumph. Neighbours stepped out of their homes and into the street to see what all the fuss was and incredulity swept the street as Catus Pompilius passed them by in his newly obtained synthesis and pileus, smiling at each and every one of them and shouting Io Saturnalia!

They arrived at the domus and Catus introduced his followers to the blessed Gorgon upon his door, swearing that he would never part from it.

Once in the atrium, the smell of fresh bread swirled

about him as he gave instruction for the youths to lay down their loads.

Ida came running in to see so many satchels and baskets that she did not know which way to turn upon her heels.

Catus waved to her and smiled before going into his tablinum and coming out with coins for each of his helpers.

The group left the domus more pleased than any previous visitor had cause to, but it would certainly not be the last, Catus told himself, for the feeling of seeing their faces so filled with happiness was something he would never get bored of. When they had all gone, Catus turned to Ida who stood alone amid all the bundles and satchels, wine amphora, delectables and more.

In that moment, however, Catus Pompilius turned to the servant he had treated with disgrace and contempt for years, and he felt shame, such shame! So much in fact that he wept as he approached her and grasped her hands before falling to his knees.

"Forgive me, please. Ida…I…have never been kind to you. You have borne my contempt with perfect courage and grace, though I did not once deserve it."

"Dominus, please," she began, feeling awkward at seeing her master kneeling before her, weeping and full of shame.

He looked up at her then, that tiny woman of supreme strength, and for the first time since they had met, she saw kindness, and caring in those eyes. A man who had been worn down by the world since the day he came into it, and she understood his life's odyssey.

"I will make it all up to you, my dear. I know what you have been through, the losses you have suffered in your life..."

Ida's hands shook as she covered her mouth, for she had never told him anything of her life, and he had never asked.

Catus nodded. "The Gods have shown me... I'm so sorry. I do not expect you to forgive me, but to accept a decision I have made." Catus stood, holding onto her hands as he rose and steadied himself. "I've decided to free you."

Truly, no sigillaria could have equalled the words Catus Pompilius uttered then, and instantly the dams of Ida's emotion cracked and her eyes flooded with unshed tears.

"Free me?" she asked.

"Yes. After the dies festus, I will go directly to the Basilica Julia and make it official. Of course…I regret that you will not be here for me to…to make things up to you, but you should not be forced to linger a moment longer."

Ida felt all manner of emotions rushing through her like quicksilver. No longer a slave? Her life her own? Where would she go? What would she do? She remembered she had no family left and that scared her more than anything. She looked at him, unsmiling, and this confused Catus.

"Are you not pleased?" he asked.

"Oh, yes, Dominus. I am. It's just that…" She did not know how to say it, but something in him recognized the absolute loneliness and fear they had in common.

"Of course…as a free woman, you can chose whichever employment you desire," Catus said, hoping against hope that she would agree to the plan he was forming. "I cannot run this home on my own. Indeed, I don't actually know how!" He laughed then, and loudly, at the absurdity of the fact. He looked around at the detritus of that domus of former beauty, and tried to imagine it alight with colour. "I would pay you a good wage, and you could choose whichever rooms you want. I would look forward to all those meals you have suggested over the years, but which I declined and -"

Ida had gathered her wits by then and grabbed hold of his hands. They both had lost everything, and they were, for better or worse, each other's familia now, though at this turn in their lives, it could only be for the better!

"I accept, sir," Ida said, nodding.

"You do?" Catus was beside himself with relief. "Thank you, Ida. Thank you." He squeezed her hands. "Io Saturnalia!" he cried and their laughter filled the atrium.

"Oh! I forgot something!" Catus ran into his tablinum and came out holding a wrapped bundle. "This…is for you." He handed her the bundle.

"For me?" Her fingers fidgeted with the strings, shaking a little, she folded back the linen and there, cradled in her arms was a brilliant pool of deep green and grey. "I…I don't know what to say."

Ida took hold of the material and a beautiful stola unfurled to the floor in front of her, just the right length, as he had described to the sellers. Ida held it to herself, and then took up the woollen cloak that went with it, dark and thick as the coarse bark of a winter oak. She knew she would never be cold in that!

"Thank you!" she said, her tears running over her lips as she laughed in gratitude to him and to the Gods themselves.

"It is my pleasure, Ida," Catus said, her happiness enough of a gift for a lifetime to him in that moment. "You must put it on, for you and I must go somewhere tonight."

"Me as well?" she asked.

"Yes!" then he stopped himself. "That is, if you would like to accompany me as my friend."

"Io Saturnalia!" she laughed, and he joined her, watching her go to her room to try it on.

Two hours later, Catus and Ida were standing before a bright red door on the Caelian hill, the old man pacing back and forth in his colourful synthesis, and she in her new stola. In addition to the new clothes, the situation in which they both found themselves was utterly foreign, and yet Saturnalia demanded that they do differently.

"Do not worry, sir," Ida reassured him. "They will be overjoyed to see you."

Catus paced more, unsure, for up until that moment he had been more certain of his new-found life of action and good will. But now, oh now, how he trembled at the thought of knocking upon that brilliant door.

Ida was beside him the next second, grasping his hand in hers. "I'll be right here with you," she whispered.

There was a great sound of raucous laughter emanating from within, so much that passers-by looked and laughed and shouted 'Io Saturnalia!'

Catus stopped shifting and nodded. "Right. Time is precious, and I've wasted enough of it. He stepped up to the door, reached out with a shaking fist, grasped the polished bronze knocker where it sat in the orbit of a great garland, and pounded three times.

The door opened, and warm light poured into the street.

"Good evening citizen," a servant dressed very much unlike a servant said. He was all smiles and had a rosy hue spread across his wide face. "Io Saturnalia!" he said, unable to withhold his laughter.

"Io Saturnalia!" Catus returned. He had made up his mind to be brave, to prostrate himself before the only person who had never given up on him, and whose opinion meant more to him than any other. "I am Catus Pompilius. I…I was invited."

The man's laughter immediately died in his throat and he began to cough most violently. When he found his breath again, he repeated, "Catus Pompilius? Dominus' uncle?"

"Yes." Catus began to think his way would be barred, his shadow too long and black to attend such a gathering, but he was wrong.

"Please…please, sir. Enter." The slave bowed low as he opened the door wide and stood aside for Catus and Ida to enter.

Ida followed Catus into the atrium, distinctly uncomfortable and unused to such surroundings.

The domus was lit by a thousand and more cerei, and colourful frescoes covered every wall. Beyond was the garden, Catus remembered from his time with Bacchus, and everywhere he looked he spied men and women drinking and singing and laughing.

"Please wait here, sir, while I get the dominus," the man said, bustling off through the crowd and leaving Catus and Ida standing there beside the glittering impluvium.

It was not long before the crowd of guests parted

and a silence fell upon the gathering. There, hurrying through them, wearing a synthesis of most extraordinary colour with a matching pileus, was Julian, accompanied by his loving wife, Viola, resplendent in a stola of red and gold.

Julian's eyes were wide in utter disbelief, and as he walked, Viola grasped his hand tightly as if to lend him strength.

"Uncle?" Julian slowed just before Catus and stopped, unable to come closer. His lip trembled momentarily, his eyes glazing the way his mother's did so long ago.

Catus stepped forward to meet his nephew, his head bowed, his pileus crushed in his old hands. "You...you invited me to your banquet yesterday."

"Yes," Julian whispered. "You came?"

Catus nodded. He knew he needed to say it now, or forever regret it, no matter the mass of people watching and listening.

"Yes... I...I'm so sorry, my nephew. Can you ever forgive me for how I have treated you? May the Gods strike me down for it..."

There was pain in the young man's eyes, true and pure sadness, before he spoke. "Strike you down?

Uncle, the Gods bless us this night!" he said before rushing in and wrapping his arms about Catus.

If Catus had not travelled the length of that dread road the Gods had shown him the previous night, then that moment could not have been anything but a dream. So great a rift mended with a few warm and welcoming words. But as he held on for dear life to his sister's son, both of them shaking with emotion, he knew with certainty that all was well, and would be so.

"Io Saturnalia!" the guests shouted behind them where not a dry eye was to be seen.

"Io Saturnalia!" Julian cried from the depts of his soul as he gazed upon his uncle at arm's length. "I'm so happy."

"Me too, my boy," Catus said, wiping his eyes. "Me too."

Julian sniffed and turned to take Viola's hand. "Uncle…this is my wife, Viola."

The young Etruscan woman stepped forward, her eyes direct and beaming with joy. "You bring great joy to our home, Catus Pompilius. The Gods smile this day!" she said, kissing him on both cheeks.

"I'm happy to meet you, my dear. And I must also beg your forgiveness for the way I have behaved. For not attending your wedding, for not-"

"Uncle," Viola said softly and kindly. "What matters is that you are here now, and our home is the merrier for it. Come. The meal is about to be served, and we have a couch reserved for you."

"Yes!" Julian cried. "We do."

Catus turned to Ida who had stood silent to that point, and took her hand. "Ida has come with me too."

"And she is very welcome!" Julian stepped past Catus, took Ida's hands and kissed them. "The Gods love you, lady!" he said.

Ida smiled, her hands ceasing to tremble as Julian led her to the triclinium after Viola and Catus.

As they walked, Catus greeted all the other guests and relief spread amongst them like a healing salve.

When they entered the triclinium, the scents, colours and sounds of Saturnalia hung about them. It might well have been the halls of Olympus for all its beauty.

Ida was shown to a plush couch where she could speak with other guests. She nestled down and found herself served wine and warm food from great steaming platters, more than she could eat to fill her small frame.

Julian had tried to insist that she sit at the lectus medius with his uncle for all her loyalty, but she insisted that she wanted Catus to have it to himself, for he had fought hard for that night she suspected.

Julian nodded, kissed her hands in great gratitude, and made his way to his own couch beside the lectus medius.

Catus reclined awkwardly upon it and found a comfortable position among the plush pillows. His silver plate was filled with meat and cheese and so much more, his cup filled brimming with rich red Etrurian wine.

Once everyone was served, Julian raised his cup to all there present and pouring out into the peristylium. His smile was one of godly joy, and everyone felt the life and hope in it. His eyes rested last upon Catus, and they all shouted together.

"Io Saturnalia!"

The Gods could not have been more pleased at the sight.

On the fourth day of Saturnalia, after the dies festus were finished, Catus Pompilius was walking joyfully about the perimeter of his own peristylium, watching the fresh crew of workmen arriving with their tools and implements to begin the great task of renovation and reinvigoration to the bones of that noble domus.

Catus encouraged them all in their work and found them well up to the task of labouring, especially in the employ of such an amenable fellow and his free woman who was filling the home with delectable scents from the kitchen.

In truth, Catus had been mulling over what he would say to Giles Amadea who was now quite late on the day he was supposed to arrive early. He chuckled as a thought came to him, a plan that was positively Saturnalian.

The truth was that Giles Amadea was not accidentally late. He had been walking the streets of Rome since early that morning, thinking about the more profitable offer he had received to make an appearance in not one, not two, but in the gladiatorial games of three public festivals in the coming weeks.

The thought had terrified him at first, for he had never wanted to set foot upon the amphitheatre sands again. However, his family was suffering, and Catus Pompilius had never paid him his worth. If he could survive the three games, then his family would not need to worry about rent, or food, or being able to pay for a much-needed medicus for his little Paulus.

He had just come from the procurator's office where he had left word with the secretary that he would accept the offer to fight. The procurator had been away, and Giles was told to return later to sign the contract.

He was now marching up the hill of the Esquiline to Catus Pompilius' dreaded domus for what he believed was the last time. No more would he have to deal with the cursed miser. As he walked, he knew his only regret would be to leave Ida to herself there, but he also knew he needed to care for his family, for they meant the entire world to him, more than his own life.

Giles arrived at the domus, but wondered if he had taken a wrong turn while lost in his thoughts, for fresh paint was being applied to the street-facing wall, and the sound of men's voices and hammering emanated from inside. But he had indeed come to the right place, and went in through the open door.

He stopped as if struck, for the place was bright with fresh paint and garlands that had been hung in honour of the season. A woman in a long wool grey cloak swept across the garden, and it was a few moments before Giles realized it was Ida.

"What's happening here?" he said aloud, and the

hammering stopped, as did Ida in her tracks.

She turned and began to approach him, her entire face a brilliant sun of joy as she came, but before she could reach him, Catus' gnarled voice grumbled from the tablinum, making Ida's smile vanish.

Giles motioned for Ida to stay where she was as he turned to go directly into Catus' office. No more would he be abused by the old wretch!

"What is the meaning of this?" Catus said, slamming his fists upon the table top and gazing up at Giles. "You're late!"

"Yes," Giles said. "I am. And I have something to tell you, Catus Pompilius!" Giles stood his ground before the wide table, and put his fists upon the scrolls and papers there spread about. "I have worked for you for years now, and I was grateful for the employment for a time. But I'm through with you…you miserable, evil man! Do you hear me?" Giles' great chest heaved as he struggled to release all the emotion he felt then without simply reaching across and choking Catus to death, for all their sakes.

Catus Pompilius stood slowly, his eyes full of life and ready for a fight. He nodded and crossed his arms as if in a court of law looking down on an accused.

"Grateful? Really!" Catus walked slowly around the table and stood before Giles. "You have no idea." He shook his head. "You dare to come here late? To shout at me? I, who have been nothing but cruel and unfeeling to you for all your hard work?"

Giles stood back a moment, trying to register the words he had just heard, suspecting foul play.

Catus' face softened then, unable to maintain the facade of wickedness and anger he had decided to don one last time. "It is I who am grateful to you, Giles Amadea."

"You?"

"Yes!" Then Catus burst out in a jolly laugh that echoed throughout the domus and spilled into the street. He laughed so much in fact that Giles thought he might die on the spot, his face was so red! "Io Saturnalia!" Catus yelled.

Giles' fists were up for a fight with a mad man, but Catus grabbed hold of them and smiled at the man in his employ.

"I have behaved abominably to you over the years, Giles Amadea, and I am going to make it up to you."

"Make it up to me?"

"Yes! For a start, I am going to pay you three times what I have been."

"Three times?"

"Yes. You need to care for your lovely family, and if you are to do so properly, you will need more. Oh, and you will live in the tenement free of rent. After I fix it up for you, that is!"

"What?" Giles shook his head, not daring to believe all that he heard, but he saw Ida appear in the doorway, her face a vision of calm joy, of relief, and he knew some great occurrence had come to pass during those first days of Saturnalia.

"Most of all, Giles…" Catus placed his hands upon the ex-gladiator's massive shoulders. "Most of all, I will help you to take care of that precious family of yours. Especially little Paulus."

At this, Giles' face softened, and pain and worry showed, for he had been beyond hope for his little boy of late.

"I will pay for the best medici from Kos and Alexandria and here in Rome so that Paulus will be well again." Catus gripped Giles' hands tightly and most earnestly. "And he will get better, Giles. By the Gods, I'll make sure he does!"

Giles gazed at the divinely changed old man before him, and thanked the Gods for it, all of it. "I believe you," he said. "I believe you!" he shouted, grateful that he had averted signing away his life that very morning to death on the sands.

"Good," Catus said, taking up a pouch of sestercii and handing it to Giles. "Now go, and spend the day with your family, my friend. You deserve all the time you have fought for. I ask only one thing of you."

"Yes, sir. Anything!" Giles said.

"That when this domus is presentable, you and your entire family will come to dine with Ida and me here."

"I…of course, sir. Of course…" Giles was at a loss, for the maelstrom of emotion had dulled his wits, but he nodded, looking to Ida for confirmation of all that he had heard. "Thank you, sir," he said to Catus at the door. "Thank you!"

"Io Saturnalia!" Catus said as Giles walked down the street and turned to him.

"Io Saturnalia!"

Catus turned back inside and took Ida's extended hand in his. "It's a start," he said to her, his hand shaking again.

"It's more than that, sir. Much more."

Catus nodded and made his way through the atrium, along the peristylium, and into the lararium which had already been finished with fine colours and newly carved statues of the Gods. He lit a chunk of incense in the flames of the fire that had been burning there constantly and placed it upon the bowl of the carved stone altar. He knelt down and raised his hands to the images of Vesta, Bacchus, Saturn and others.

"Thank you Gods… With all of my heart and soul, I thank you."

From that day forward, the name of Catus Pompilius was synonymous with goodwill and hope across all of Rome, for all believed that he was indeed blessed by the Gods.

There was not a Saturnalia in which his charity was not mentioned, nor a gathering in which his jolly, aged face was not recommended to the Gods. And he was said to be not only thus for the duration of that sacred festival, that best of days, but the whole of the year, from start to finish.

His family and friends blessed the day he had come back to them, especially Giles and Marcia Amadea whose tiny son, Paulus, now flourished in life, healthy and strong, and was a constant companion of the kind old man upon the Esquiline.

The people of the Suburra would never hear a harsh word spoken against the landlord who had set the standard for all others. No doubt other men of business and owners of tenements thought him mad, beyond help, but the thoughts of those less fortunate mortals were of no consequence.

Catus Pompilius felt alive, he honoured his fellow man and above all, the Gods, for they had given him back his life and taken pleasure in his metamorphosis.

Would that it could be said of all who walk the earth, and may the words of Paulus Amadea ever pass our lips as we utter them: "Io Saturnalia! May the Gods bless him!"

THE END

Thank you for reading!

Did you enjoy *Saturnalia*? Here is what you can do next.

If you enjoyed this story, and if you have a minute to spare, please post a short review on the web page where you purchased the book.

Reviews are a wonderful way for new readers to find this book and your help in spreading the word is greatly appreciated.

More exciting historical fantasy from Eagles and Dragons Publishing will be coming soon, so be sure to sign-up for e-mail updates at:

www.eaglesanddragonspublishing.com

Newsletter subscribers get a FREE BOOK, and first access to new releases, special offers, and much more!

BECOME A PATRON OF EAGLES AND DRAGONS PUBLISHING!

If you enjoy the books that Eagles and Dragons Publishing puts out, our blogs about history, mythology, and archaeology, our video tours of historic sites and more, then you should consider becoming an official patron.

We love our regular visitors to the website, and of course our wonderful newsletter subscribers, but we want to offer more to our 'super fans', those readers and history-lovers who enjoy everything we do and create.

You can become a patron for as little as $1 per month. For your support, you will also get loads of fantastic rewards as tokens of our appreciation.

If you are interested, just visit the website below to go to the Eagles and Dragons Publishing Patreon page to watch the introductory video and check out the patronage levels and exciting rewards.

https://www.patreon.com/EaglesandDragonsPublishing

Join us for an exciting future as we bring the past to life!

AUTHOR'S NOTE

Charles Dickens' *A Christmas Carol* is, to me, one of the most perfect stories ever formulated, or told. I read it every year at Christmastime, and I never tire of it. How many stories can one read, and re-read, and still feel the full impact of emotion conveyed within the text?

In a way, *Saturnalia* is my homage to this great storytelling tradition.

At first, I was reluctant to undertake this project. I thought it a little foolhardy and presumptive. Who am I to follow in Mr. Dickens' footsteps? But then I started to think about the tale in the context of ancient Rome which is, after all, the world in which I 'live' most of the time.

I felt a huge burden before starting, of course. Such titanic footsteps to follow! But then I started to really enjoy the research and the creation of this story in the context of ancient Rome. I clung to the carved image of Cato the Elder, a stern representation of Roman values and Republicanism, and thought that if I could succeed in taking that man on an odyssey of change, then perhaps it could work. The trick was to bring the world of ancient Rome to life, the same as in my other books, and that is partly the reason I set it during the reign of Septimius Severus. That is, after all, a period of Rome's history with which I am very familiar. For the most part, I stayed true to the story of Dickens' original manuscript, but there were times when I felt a bit more was needed for the context, hence Catus' journey to the Underworld, a place of true horror for anyone in the ancient world.

It is said that many of our Christmas traditions do indeed come from the Roman festival of Saturnalia - things such as the burning of candles, the giving of gifts (*sigillaria*), the hanging of holly and ivy, and much more. I won't go into a history of this ancient Roman festival, but if you would like to learn more about it, you can read the article, *Io Saturnalia! – Celebrating the Best of Days in Ancient Rome*, on the Eagles and Dragons Publishing website.

As ever with my books, I hope that this has both entertained and educated the reader. The world of ancient Rome is endlessly fascinating to me, and I do indeed hope that I have done justice to it once more, its great symphony of colour, sights, sounds and beliefs.

My hope is that, when one reads this story at Christmastime, or any other time, you are pulled back in history to a time when there were good people, and bad people, those with means and those without, a time when people truly believed the gods had a hand in their everyday lives, for they believed this fervently. They celebrated their gods and the lives they had been given, even in the face of pain and suffering.

Perhaps in reading this, we might examine our own lives and realize that sometimes, this wonder-filled life may not be as dire as it seems.

Thank you for reading.

Adam Alexander Haviaras

Toronto, 2018

GLOSSARY

acetum - wine of the poorer classes, a thick, vinegary syrup mixed with water to form wine

aedes – a temple; sometimes a room

aedituus – a keeper of a temple

aestivus – relating to summer; a summer camp or pasture

agora – Greek word for the central gathering place of a city or settlement

ala – an auxiliary cavalry unit

amita – an aunt

amphitheatre – an oval or round arena where people enjoyed gladiatorial combat and other spectacles

anguis – a dragon, serpent or hydra; also used to refer to the 'Draco' constellation

angusticlavius – 'narrow stripe' on a tunic; Lucius Metellus Anguis is a *tribunus angusticlavius*

apodyterium – the changing room of a bath house

aquila – a legion's eagle standard which was made

of gold during the Empire

aquilifer – senior standard bearer in a Roman legion who carried the legion's eagle

ara – an altar

armilla – an arm band that served as a military decoration

as - a bronze coin; 400 asses = 1 gold aureus approx.

atrium – unroofed entrance room of a Roman house, usually containing a pool, or impluvium

augur – a priest who observes natural occurrences to determine if omens are good or bad; a soothsayer

aureus – a Roman gold coin; worth twenty-five silver *denarii*

auriga – a charioteer

ballista – an ancient missile-firing weapon that fired either heavy 'bolts' or rocks

bireme – a galley with two banks of oars on either side

bracae – knee or full-length breeches originally

worn by barbarians but adopted by the Romans

caldarium – the 'hot' room of a bath house; from the Latin *calidus*

caligae – military shoes or boots with or without hobnail soles

cardo – a hinge-point or central, north-south thoroughfare in a fort or settlement, the *cardo maximus*

castrum – a Roman fort

cataphract – a heavy cavalryman; both horse and rider were armoured

cena- the principal, afternoon meal of the Romans

centurion – a Roman officer who commanded a century of 80 men; centurions were usually career soldiers

cerei - candles, usually of tallow or bees wax

chiton – a long woollen tunic of Greek fashion

chryselephantine – ancient Greek sculptural medium using gold and ivory; used for cult statues

cingulum – a belt or harness

civica – relating to 'civic'; the civic crown was awarded to one who saved a Roman citizen in war

civitas – a settlement or commonwealth; an administrative centre in tribal areas of the Empire

clepsydra – a water clock

cognomen – the surname of a Roman which distinguished the branch of a gens

collegia – an association or guild; e.g. *collegium pontificum* means 'college of priests'

colonia – a colony; also used for a farm or estate

consul – an honorary position in the Empire; during the Republic they presided over the Senate

contubernium – a military unit of eight men within a century who shared a tent

contus – a long cavalry spear; sometimes spelled 'kontus'

convivium publicum - a public feast paid for by the state

corbita – a type of large hold merchant ship

cornicen – the horn blower in a legion

cornu – a curved military horn

cornucopia – the horn of plenty

corona – a crown; often used as a military decoration

cubiculum – a bedchamber

cursus honorum - the course of honour; a specific career path for upper class Roman men

curia – the Senate building in the Roman Forum

curule – refers to the chair upon which Roman magistrates would sit (e.g. *curule aedile*)

decumanus – refers to the tenth; the *decumanus maximus* ran east to west in a Roman fort or city

denarius – A Roman silver coin; worth one hundred brass *sestertii*

dies festus - holidays in ancient Rome, or literally 'festival days'

dignitas – a Roman's worth, honour and reputation

dominus - the master of a household; female is 'domina'

domus – a home or house

draco – a military standard in the shape of a dragon's head first used by Sarmatians and adopted by Rome

draconarius – a military standard bearer who held the draco

duplicarius – trooper with special skills who receives double-pay (ex. an engineer)

eques – a horseman or rider

equites – cavalry; of the order of knights in ancient Rome

fabrica – a workshop

fabula – an untrue or mythical story; a play or drama

familia – a Roman's household, including slaves

fascies – double-headed axes bound in reeds and carried by lictors who followed senior officials

flammeum – a flame-coloured bridal veil

forum – an open square or marketplace; also a place of public business (e.g. the *Forum Romanum*) fossa – a ditch or trench; a part of defensive earthworks

frigidarium – the 'cold room' of a bath house; a cold plunge pool

funeraticia – from *funereus* for funeral; the *collegia funeraticia* assured all received decent burial

garum – a fish sauce that was very popular in the Roman world

gens humanum – the human race; gens means clan

gladius – a Roman short sword

gorgon – a terrifying visage of a woman with snakes for hair; also known as Medusa

greaves – armoured shin and knee guards worn by high-ranking officers

groma – a surveying instrument; used for accurately marking out towns, marching camps and forts etc.

hasta – a spear or javelin

hastile – a staff with a large orb on one end, carried by an optio heptastadion – a causeway built to connect Alexandria to the island of Pharos; seven stades long

hetaira – a courtesan; different from a common prostitute, or lupa

horreum – a granary

hydraulis – a water organ

hypocaust – area beneath a floor in a home or bath house that is heated by a furnace

images – standards that bore the image of the emperor and were carried with the legionary standards

imperator – a commander or leader; commander-in-chief

impluvium – the pool in a household atrium that was open to the sky and caught rain water

insula – a block of flats leased to the poor

intervallum – the space between two palisades

itinere – a road or itinerary; the journey

lanista – a gladiator trainer

lararium - the household shrine to the gods in a Roman home

lectus medius - the seat of honour in a Roman dining room

lemure – a ghost

libellus – a little book or diary

lituus – the curved staff or wand of an augur; also a cavalry trumpet

lorica – body armour; can be made of mail, scales or metal strips; can also refer to a cuirass

ludus - a gladiator school; example is the 'Ludus Magnus' in Rome

lupa – a common prostitute; lupa literally means 'she-wolf'

lupanar – a brothel; example is the 'Great Lupanar' of Pompeii

lustratio – a ritual purification, usually involving a sacrifice

manica – handcuffs; also refers to the long sleeves of a tunic marita – wife

maritus – husband

matertera – a maternal aunt

maximus – meaning great or 'of greatness'

medicus – a doctor; army field doctor

missum – used as a call for mercy by the crowd for a gladiator who had fought bravely

mola salsa - salted flour or grains used in religious sacrifices

murmillo – a heavily armed gladiator with a helmet, shield and sword

nomen – the *gens* of a family (as opposed to *cognomen* which was the specific branch of a wider *gens*)

nones – the fifth day of every month in the Roman calendar

novendialis – refers to the ninth day

nutrix – a wet-nurse or foster mother

nymphaeum – a pool, fountain or other monument

dedicated to the nymphs

officium – an official employment; also a sense of duty or respect

onager – a powerful catapult used by the Romans; named after a wild ass because of its kick

optio – the officer beneath a centurion; second-in-command within a century

palaestra – the open space of a gymnasium where wrestling, boxing and other such events were practiced

palliatus – indicating someone clad in a pallium

pancration – a no-holds-barred sport that combined wrestling and boxing

parentalis – of parents or ancestors; (e.g. *Parentalia* was a festival in honour of the dead)

parma – a small, round shield often used by light-armed troops; also referred to as *parmula*

pater – a father

pax – peace; a state of peace as opposed to war

peregrinus – a strange or foreign person or thing

peristylum – a peristyle; a colonnade around a building; can be inside or outside of a building or home

phalerae – decorative medals or discs worn by centurions or other officers on the chest

pileus - a felt or leather skull cap worn by men during the festival of Saturnalia

pilum – a heavy javelin used by Roman legionaries

plebeius – of the plebeian class or the people

pontifex – a Roman high priest

popa – a junior priest or temple servant

primus pilus – the senior centurion of a legion who commanded the first cohort

pronaos – the porch or entrance to a building such as a temple

protome – an adornment on a work of art, usually a frontal view of an animal

pteruges – protective leather straps used on armour; often a leather skirt for officers

pugio – a dagger

quadriga – a four-horse chariot

quinqueremis – a ship with five banks of oars

retiarius – a gladiator who fights with a net and trident

ritus Graecus - literally means 'in the Greek rite' - performing a religious sacrifice with one's head uncovered

rosemarinus – the herb rosemary

rudus – a heavy wooden *gladius* or sword used for practice and to build strength

rusticus – of the country; e.g. a *villa rustica* was a country villa

sacrum – sacred or holy; e.g. the *Via Sacra* or 'sacred way'

salii – the dancing priests of Mars who performed ritual dances in Rome's streets during the Festival of Mars

schola – a place of learning and learned discussion;

plural 'scholae'

scutum – the large, rectangular, curved shield of a legionary

secutor – a gladiator armed with a sword and shield; often pitted against a *retiarius*

sestertius – a Roman silver coin worth a quarter *denarius*

sica – a type of dagger

sigillaria - small token gifts given during the festival of Saturnalia; examples are candles or dice

signum – a military standard or banner

signifer – a military standard bearer

sistrum – an ancient instrument or rattle made up of tiny cymbals

spatha – an auxiliary trooper's long sword; normally used by cavalry because of its longer reach

spina – the ornamented, central median in stadiums such as the *Circus Maximus* in Rome

stadium – a measure of length approximately 607 feet; also refers to a race course

stibium – *antimony*, which was used for dyeing

eyebrows by women in the ancient world

stoa – a columned, public walkway or portico for public use; often used by merchants to sell their wares

stola – a long outer garment worn by Roman women

strigilis – a curved scraper used at the baths to remove oil and grime from the skin

stylus – a bronze or wood 'pen' used to write with ink on papyrus, or on wax tablets

synthesis - a colourful patchwork robe or tunic worn by men during the festival of Saturnalia

taberna – an inn or tavern

tablinum – an office or work space where documents are stored and business is conducted

tabula – a Roman board game similar to backgammon; also a writing-tablet for keeping records

tepidarium – the 'warm room' of a bath house

tessera – a piece of mosaic paving; a die for playing; also a small wooden plaque

testudo – a tortoise formation created by troops'

interlocking shields

thraex – a gladiator in Thracian armour

tibicen - flute player present at religious sacrifices

titulus – a title of honour or honourable designation

torques – also 'torc'; a neck band worn by Celtic peoples and adopted by Rome as a military decoration

trepidatio – trepidation, anxiety or alarm

tribunus – a senior officer in an imperial legion; there were six per legion, each commanding a cohort

triclinium – a dining room

trierarchus – the captain of a ship or fleet

tunica – a sleeved garment worn by both men and women

ustrinum – the site of a funeral pyre

vallum – an earthen wall or rampart with a palisade

veterinarius – a veterinary surgeon in the Roman army

vexillarius – a Roman standard bearer who carried the *vexillum* for each unit

vexillum – a standard carried in each unit of the Roman army

victimarius - the person who performed the actual slaughter of the animal during religious sacrifices

vicus – a settlement of civilians living outside a Roman fort

vigiles – Roman firemen; literally 'watchmen'

vinerod – a stick, or short staff, carried by a centurion that gave him the right to strike citizens

vitis – the twisted 'vinerod' of a Roman centurion; a centurion's emblem of office

vittae – a ribbon or band

ACKNOWLEDGMENTS

It always feels strange to come to this part of the creative process, the time when I acknowledge all the people who have had a positive effect upon the creation of a work. There are always too many to name, people who have helped indirectly through the smallest interaction, be it in person or virtual.

It feels stranger still, for the first person I acknowledge to be someone who is long dead. However, without his story, this one would not have come to pass. I am speaking, of course, of Mr. Charles Dickens. I have enjoyed *A Christmas Carol* for most of my life. At first it was by way of films and children's picture books, and then the original work itself. I never tire of the story in its many incarnations and retellings. *Saturnalia* is, partially, my own thank you to Mr. Dickens whose shade, it could be said, sat by me as I wrote my homage to his timeless tale.

But there are many others to thank as well.

I would be remiss without offering my sincere thanks to all my readers who constantly send me notes of encouragement. No matter how confident a person is, the kind words of those who enjoy the work make the process that much more fulfilling. A special shout-out should go to my patrons too, especially Bonnie, whose kindness and reassurance for every book release has been ongoing.

I would also like to acknowledge my fellow historians and archaeologists across various social media groups who share and encourage my love of the ancient world, and who possess the will to preserve and promote it. You're all champions of history!

No book can be a success without a wonderful cover, and so, once more, I would like to thank my brilliant cover designer, Laura at LLPix Designs, who makes that part of the creative process a true joy. Thank you for being so wonderful to work with!

It is also a certainty that no book can be a success without a good editorial crew, and so I would like to offer my heartfelt thanks to both Angelina and Jeanette at Eagles and Dragons Publishing for their tireless work in reading and reviewing every work I produce. Thank you for making me bleed and weep, ladies, for my work is the better for it.

Lastly, I would like to thank my entire family, to whom this book is dedicated. Their love, encouragement, and support over the course of writing this book, and every other book I write, is immeasurable. They are my light in the dark.

Apart from being a story of wickedness and redemption, *Saturnalia* is also a story about family, what it means to have one, and the void that is left when one does not. In writing this book, I was reminded at every turn how empty my life would be without them.

Adam Alexander Haviaras

Toronto, 2018

ABOUT THE AUTHOR

Adam Alexander Haviaras is a writer and historian who has studied ancient and medieval history and archaeology in Canada and the United Kingdom. He currently resides in Toronto with his wife and children where he is continuing his research and writing other works of historical fantasy.

Historical Fiction/Fantasy Titles

The Eagles and Dragons Series

The Dragon: Genesis (Prequel)

A Dragon among the Eagles (Prequel)

Children of Apollo (Book I)

Killing the Hydra (Book II)

Warriors of Epona (Book III)

Isle of the Blessed (Book IV)

The Stolen Throne (Book V)

The Blood Road (Book VI)

The Carpathian Interlude Series

Immortui (Part I)

Lykoi (Part II)

Thanatos (Part III)

The Mythologia Series

Chariot of the Son

Heart of Fire: A Novel of the Ancient Olympics

Saturnalia: A Tale of Wickedness and Redemption in Ancient Rome

Short Stories

The Sea Released

Theoi

Nex (or, The Warrior Named for Death)

Titles in the *Historia* Non-fiction Series

Historia I: Celtic Literary Archetypes in *The Mabinogion*: A Study of the Ancient Tale of *Pwyll, Lord of Dyved*

Historia II: Arthurian Romance and the Knightly Ideal: A study of Medieval Romantic Literature and its Effect upon Warrior Culture in Europe

Historia III: *Y Gododdin*: The Last Stand of Three Hundred Britons - Understanding People and Events during Britain's Heroic Age

Historia IV: Camelot: The Historical, Archaeological and Toponymic Considerations for South Cadbury Castle as King Arthur's Capital

Eagles and Dragons Publishing Guides

Writing the Past: The Eagles and Dragons Publishing Guide to Researching, Writing, Publishing and Marketing Historical Fiction and Historical Fantasy

STAY CONNECTED

To connect with Adam and learn more about the ancient world visit:
www.eaglesanddragonspublishing.com

Sign up for the Eagles and Dragons Publishing Newsletter at www.eaglesanddragonspublishing.com/newsletter-join-the-legions/ to receive a FREE BOOK, first access to new releases and posts on ancient history, special offers, and much more!

Readers can also connect with Adam on Twitter @AdamHaviaras and Instagram @ adam_haviaras.

On Facebook you can 'Like' the Eagles and Dragons page to get regular updates on new historical fiction and non-fiction from Eagles and Dragons Publishing.

Printed in Poland
by Amazon Fulfillment
Poland Sp. z o.o., Wrocław

51009501R00155